PIGmalion

by Mark Dunn

A SAMUEL FRENCH ACTING EDITION

SAMUEL
FRENCH

FOUNDED 1830

NEW YORK HOLLYWOOD LONDON TORONTO

SAMUELFRENCH.COM

ISBN 978-0-573-69804-0   Printed in U.S.A.   #29275

MUSIC USE NOTE

IMPORTANT BILLING AND CREDIT
REQUIREMENTS

PIGmalion opened at the Community Theatre League in Williamsport, Pennsylvania on October 17, 2008. The director was Tom Ryersbach. The stage manager and props manager was Sandy Dougherty. The assistant stage manager was Georgia Coffey. The production manager was Holly Patton Shull. The technical director was Ed Richards. The assistant technical director was Joe Moyer. The set was constructed by Joe Moyer, George Kulp and Steve Soha under the direction of Mr. Moyer. The costumes were by Sandie Fairman. The wardrobe mistress was Nancy Reiff. The properties chiefs were Glenn and Molly Blakeslee. Makeup was by Denise Gray. The set projection artists were Casey Glaghorn and Brian Lutz. The stage crew included Janiece Katherman, Cydne Shull and Alisa Bugorova. The cast, in order of appearance, was:

FAIRGOERS. . . . . Susan Guinter, Tim Mallery, Cheryl Appleton,
W. Joseph Falk

FREDDY HILL. . . . . Thomas Powell

CLARA HILL . . . . Alison Malee

IDA HILL. . . . . Sandie Fairman

HENRY HIGGINS . . . . Conrad Shull

CAL PICKERING. . . . . Ted Cockley

ELIZA DOOLITTLE. . . . . Leanne Brown

TIFFANY BOX . . . . Stephen Furey

OPAL. . . . . Cheryl Appleton

VICKI HILL. . . . . Christie Heimbach

WAITRESS . . . . Susan Guinter

WAITER. . . . . Tim Mallery

GERALD . . . . Tim Mallery

CHARACTERS

FAIRGOERS – A YOUNG MAN* and **YOUNG WOMAN***
 AN OLDER MAN* and **OLDER WOMAN***

FREDDY HILL – a young man in his twenties

CLARA HILL – a young woman in her twenties, Freddy's sister

IDA HILL – Freddy and Clara's mother

HENRY HIGGINS – a college professor in his late forties

CAL PICKERING – also a college professor in his late forties, and Henry's colleague and friend

ELIZA DOOLITTLE – a pig farmer's daughter in her twenties

TIFFANY BOX – a drag queen of indeterminate age, and Eliza's best friend

OPAL* – Ida Hill's maid

VICKI HILL – Ida Hill's third child; like her siblings, also in her twenties

A RESTAURANT HOSTESS*

A WAITER*

CHAD* – a different waiter and former student of Cal Pickering

GERALD* – a bartender and pool-boy

*Double-casting possibilities

TIME AND PLACE

The play takes place in the fall of this year in various locations within the fictional southern city of Shawsville, Mississippi.

A WORD ABOUT THE SET

The six scenes that make up *PIGmalion* were written for representative staging. That is to say, the play is best presented through a series of suggestive sets that are created through set pieces and furniture that move easily on and off (for the purpose of quick scene changes) or convert from one thing to another. Indeed, the script directs that the action of scene three of the second act should move from one place to another: from the classroom to the bar and back and forth between the bar and the Hill family terrace. Such fluidity of action would be difficult to effect with ponderous, locked-down sets.

Although the play should not be staged in such a minimalist fashion as to lose the color and flavor of its southern milieu, it isn't necessary to overdress. It is the characters that tell the story – not the set.

Dedicated to my favorite family of Mississippi thespians,
The Hays,
Tonya, Rick, Aubrey and Gracie,
and to all my friends in the Mississippi Theatre Association.

ACT ONE

Scene One

(Lights come up on the main fairgrounds concourse of the Tri-Counties Fair and Livestock Show in Shawsville, Mississippi. We are in the midst of this year's early autumn festivities. Much is indicated by pulsating colored lights and the sounds of the midway. Downstage are three picnic tables, two of which are occupied by fairgoing **COUPLES** *eating hamburgers: a young male and female* **COUPLE** *and an older male and female* **COUPLE**. *There is a directional sign upstage that sends fairgoers either to the Quilts and Comforters competition or to the "Catch a Greased Pig" contest. The* **OLDER MAN**'s *attention is suddenly captured by something offstage. He gets to his feet.)*

OLDER MAN. *(calling offstage)* Cooter! Cooter, boy, I'm not gonna tell you again: stop it right now or we're goin' home!

(He sits back down.)

OLDER WOMAN. What's he doin'?

OLDER MAN. Makin' faces at people – at ever-body that passes.

(The **OLDER WOMAN** *now stands up to get her own better view. She gives her unseen son a good look and then sits back down and returns to her burger.)*

OLDER WOMAN. He ain't makin' faces, honey.

OLDER MAN. Yes he is.

OLDER WOMAN. No he ain't, darlin'. That's just the way he looks.

(The **OLDER MAN** *gets up and takes another look, then sits down.)*

OLDER MAN. We got ugly kids, Eunice.

OLDER WOMAN. Eat your hamburger, Travis.

(A moment passes. Two women and a man enter from the direction of the Quilts competition. The man, **FREDDY HILL,** *and his sister,* **CLARA HILL,** *are both in their twenties, dressed in that casual, yet stylish way that moneyed young people often effect. The other woman, older by two or three decades, is* **IDA,** *their mother. She is also dressed well, perhaps too nice for a visit to the Tri-Counties Fair and Livestock Show.* **IDA** *goes to the unoccupied picnic table and sits down. She takes off a shoe and gingerly begins to massage her big toe.)*

CLARA. How's the foot, Mama? Are you in pain?

IDA. It isn't the whole foot, honey – just the big toe. It throbs. It also feels like somebody's using it for a pin-cushion.

FREDDY. *(to* **IDA***)* The next time Clara and I take you to the fair, we're setting you up in one of those motorized carts.

IDA. Carts?

(to **CLARA***)*

What's your brother talking about?

CLARA. I think he means those little thingees disabled people zip up and down the aisles at K-Mart in.

IDA. I'd sooner drink poison.

CLARA. Why don't you drink a little black cherry juice instead? It really *is* supposed to work, Mama. Just a few ounces a day they say, and your gout'll be gone forever.

IDA. *Who* says this? Did you get this out of one of those alternative lifestyle magazines of yours?

CLARA. *(shaking her head)* It was *Prevention,* Mama.

IDA. Oh. Well. I just –

(mock-confidentially to **FREDDY***)*

IDA. *(cont.)* She forces me to drink wheat grass smoothies. When no one's around to knock them out of her hand.

(to **CLARA**, *while patting her hand)*

Although I do appreciate your concern. You're a good daughter.

(looking about)

Where's your sister?

CLARA. She left.

IDA. What do you mean, she left? This was supposed to be a family outing.

CLARA. Some woman who looked like Grandma Moses started accosting her.

IDA. What are you talking about?

FREDDY. You know how old ladies tend to gravitate to Vicki. They get this odd notion in their heads that she's – I don't know – *approachable.*

CLARA. When in actuality old people give Vicki hives. Old people, poor people. The disabled. She fled, Mama. She couldn't get herself out of the family arts building fast enough.

IDA. Does she ever flee from *me?* When my back is turned? Do I ever make her want to run for her car?

FREDDY. You're not old, Mom. Or at least you're doing a good job of keeping yourself up.

IDA. *(suspiciously)* I don't know if I should take that as a compliment or an insult.

(thought shift)

Freddy, honey, if this pain doesn't subside, I may not be able to make it across the parking lot.

(She winces.)

Could you perhaps bring the car around to that exit gate over there?

(pointing)

Are we ready to go, Clara? Have we gotten our fill of country quilts for one afternoon?

CLARA. *(disappointed)* Didn't you like the quilts?

IDA. They were lovely, sweetie. The designs were beautiful, the craftsmanship, the stitching – it was all wonderful. I'm so glad we came. You know, it's sad to think that we have so few outings like this anymore – not since your father died. Freddy, are *you* ready to go?

FREDDY. *(He isn't ready.)* Sure. Okay.

IDA. You're *not*, are you?

FREDDY. No, it's fine. We can go.

IDA. *(sincere)* I'm spoiling your fun, aren't I?

FREDDY. No you're not.

IDA. Yes I am.

FREDDY. You're not, Mom – *really.*

IDA. I most certainly am. I can see the disappointment in your face.

FREDDY. *(touching his face)* There's no disappointment in my face.

CLARA. *(on the verge of a scream)* If you two don't stop this right now, I'm marching over to that hot dog stand and turn myself back into your fat daughter.

IDA. *(to **FREDDY**)* Freddy, I can sit right here until you and Clara have seen all of the fair that you want to. Clara, honey, would you like to see more of the fair? We never come. We should come more often. I wouldn't call it slumming at all.

FREDDY. Who said it was slumming?

IDA. Your other sister.

CLARA. Yes, I can picture Vicki saying something like that.

IDA. She's doing the best she can. Vicki can't help it that she was born…

CLARA. *(finishing for her)* …with a silver spoon stuck up her butt.

(**FREDDY** *laughs.* **IDA** *wags a finger at her daughter, but smiles in spite of herself.*)

IDA. Well, she's gone now, so why don't the two of you trot on over to the midway and throw some balls at something?

FREDDY. *(trying unsuccessfully to hide his eagerness)* Maybe for a few minutes.

(He kisses his mother on the cheek as does **CLARA.** *The two dash off. They nearly collide with two men in their late forties,* **HENRY HIGGINS** *and* **CAL PICKERING.** *There is an academic, observational air about them.* **HENRY** *is scribbling in a notebook. They make their way over to the picnic tables.)*

CAL. *(to* **HENRY***)* Don't you ever stop working?

HENRY. How would I do that, Cal? Plug up my ears? Autonomous intake, Calvin; I'm a helpless prisoner to it.

CAL. You should set up a booth. Like that "guess your weight" pitchman over there.

HENRY. So instead of estimating a person's age or weight, I'd be the slightly tweedy barker who guesses where the rube *came* from.

CAL. Exactly. For my money watching some professorial type pegging people's provenances would be an appreciably more pleasurable pasttime than putting –

HENRY. *(interrupting, a criticism)* Cal, you're alliterating again.

CAL. I am?

HENRY. Yes.

CAL. Sorry. All I'm saying is that you would be really good at it.

HENRY. Of course, it doesn't matter, does it, that you have a slight bias here?

CAL. Bias? Because I'm your friend?

HENRY. Yes, and because you teach geography. You're *naturally* inclined to be interested in where people come from.

CAL. Fine. But I still think it's a magnificent gift you have. And maybe it's time you started using that gift for some purpose other than educational inculcation or – or those all-but-unreadable little treatises on dialect and slang you diligently self-publish.

HENRY. *(taking offense)* All but unreadable?

CAL. Except among a small, seasoned circle of scholarly semanticists and linguists.

HENRY. The alliteration, Cal: it grates.

CAL. *(ignoring this)* I'm just saying, Henry, that it would probably be fun to see *you* having some fun for a change: putting all your theories, and that vast storehouse of dialectal knowledge to some practical purpose.

HENRY. You mean like for "fun and profit"?

(CAL nods enthusiastically.)

I suppose I *could* have some fun. But how do I know that there isn't some ulterior motive behind all this flattery? How can I be sure that you aren't just buttering me up so I'll agree to pay for your...

(He does a quick study of what all the people around him are eating. He addresses the YOUNG MAN sitting at one of the two picnic tables.)

What is that?

YOUNG MAN. *(playing along, with good-natured humor)* It's called a hamburger.

HENRY. Thank you, sir.

(turning back to CAL)

Your hamburger. Hmmm?

CAL. *(a protest)* Hey, wait just a minute there, Henry. I have money.

HENRY. *(shaking his head)* Not *on* you. You underestimate my powers of observation, Professor Pickering. You spent your last dollar at the ring toss. Don't deny it.

CAL. *(poetic, acquiescing)* A prisoner to my fate: land rich but cash poor. I should liquidate a few hundred of my legacy Delta bottomland acres and treat myself to an extra game of ring toss now and then. Or miniature golf, or spend a whimsical night at the bowling lanes. 'Haven't done any of those things, Henry. Haven't even seen one of those monster truck competitions the populi are always going on about.

HENRY. Nor have I. Of course the difference here, Cal, is that I have no *desire* to. Two tractors go to pull at one another in a woods without me there to see it: was there relevance? I am content with my books and my music and my staid professorial existence, content to let my own fortune agglomerate in the vault. And there's the dirty little secret we both share and which Covent College shall never know: its linguistics and geography professors are richer than Croesus. So shall I treat us both to a hamburger or not?

CAL. Yes. But first –

HENRY. But first what?

CAL. Let's have a little fun, Henry. Let's dazzle a few of these folks by telling them exactly where they're from. They'll get a big kick out of it and so will you.

HENRY. Phonetic linguistics is a serious vocation, Cal. Not a lark.

CAL. *(noticing* IDA*)* Take *her,* for example.

HENRY. I don't want to play.

CAL. Indulge me, Henry. Now, by her garb, I'd say that this woman has some money – maybe a good deal of money – but you're not going to get much more from her unless she decides to open her mouth. And then by my calculation she need only say a sentence or two and you'll be able to place her within a fifty miles of where she was born.

HENRY. I can…but I won't.

CAL. *(playfully)* You're tempted. I see it in your face.

HENRY. My face isn't telling you any such thing.

CAL. I know you want to.

HENRY. *(relenting)* Oh for crying out loud.

(He crosses to IDA. *Addressing her.)*

Excuse me, ma'am. My friend and I were wondering if the hamburgers here are any good.

IDA. I wouldn't know. I'm just resting my foot.

HENRY. There's something wrong with your foot?

IDA. I have gout. There. The truth is out; now all the vendors in the fairgrounds will hide their veal chops and shrimp scampi from me.

(**HENRY** *and* **CAL** *laugh.* **HENRY** *turns to* **CAL**, *as* **IDA** *looks on.*)

HENRY. Born in Little Rock – *North* Little Rock. Moved at some point to Memphis. Schooled up north – Bryn Mawr would be my guess. Even sojourned in Philadelphia for a time.

(*turning back to* **IDA**)

Am I right? You've lived in Philadelphia? Society Hill or Rittenhouse Square?

IDA. (*with an expression of amazement*) Who *are* you?

HENRY. (*taking her hand to shake it*) Professor Henry Higgins.

IDA. Of Covent College?

HENRY. You're familiar with my work?

IDA. Just your name. My late husband was affiliated with the school and might have mentioned you on occasion.

HENRY. And did he ever happen to mention the name of my colleague, Professor Calvin Pickering?

IDA. (*cudgeling her brains*) Pickering? Let me think –

(**CAL** *and* **IDA** *shake hands.*)

HENRY. No relation, of course, to the Virgin Islands baseball player by that name nor to any of the illustrious statesmen and governmental men of that same surname, but, in fact, a direct descendant of William Henry Pickering, the astronomer, who discovered the tenth moon of Saturn which he called "Themis," – a most remarkable discovery…had it been true. He also distinguished himself by theorizing that the craters of the moon were attributable to lunar insects, and eventually had himself convinced that there was abundant vegetation upon that self-same satellite.

CAL. That's enough disparaging of my lineage for one afternoon, Henry.

HENRY. My friend Cal, having wisely eschewed astronomy, has turned out to be quite a fine geography instructor.

IDA. I'm sure he is. But how did you know that I've lived in Memphis *and* Philadelphia? And how on earth did you know that I was born in Little Rock?

HENRY. Your *accent*, Ms. –

IDA. Hill. Ida Hill.

CAL. *(to* IDA*)* He's very good, isn't he?

IDA. Extremely good.

(to HENRY, *getting into the spirit of the game)*

Can you do those girls over there?

HENRY. What girls?

IDA. *(pointing offstage)* The ones with the big bags, jabbering away at each other. Would you be able to tell us where *they're* from?

CAL. *(eagerly answering for Henry)* Down to the very county – just watch.

HENRY. *(to* CAL*)* You're not going to make me the trained monkey here, Cal.

CAL. No, but your put-down of my great-great grandfather was uncalled for. You owe me. Do those two vendors, Henry.

(Two young women now enter: ELIZA DOOLITTLE *and her friend* TIFFANY BOX. *TIFFANY is a drag queen. The two carry a number of bags affixed to shoulder sticks. Each bag is filled with what will soon be revealed through the dialogue: pork rinds. Both women speak in very thick and very "country" Deep-South accents, which can only be partially suggested by their scripted dialogue.)*

TIFFANY. Liza, I ain't never seen so many people deliberately lookin' in the opposite way when I come up on 'em, like I'm somebody'd make a little kid hide a-tremblin' under his danged bed, or some such foolish shit as that. I cain't say if it was me and all this new sparkle-spackle I got all over my face to hide all them hormone blemishes or if it's on account of I gotta carry around a mess of pork rinds all over the dang-dabbed fairgrounds to help out my friend Liza Jane.

ELIZA. Well, it ain't the pork rinds that's the problem, I'm sure of *that.* Ain't hardly nobody don't like the smell of fresh-fried pork rinds. And if you don't wanna help me, Tiffany, then don't help me. I didn't ask you to do it as a favor no wise anyways. You're makin' yourself a little money, ain't you?

TIFFANY. Yep, I'm makin' money, honey, but I ain't makin' any more money than I could've made standin' out behind the freak tent and lifting my wig up and down to those fellas what might be interested.

ELIZA. One of these days, Tiffany, you're gonna lift that wig to the wrong fella and he's gonna punch your danged lights out.

(They walk up to the picnic table occupied by the young **COUPLE.** *Addressing the man and woman.)*

Homemade pork rinds. Two dollars a bag.

MAN. No thank you.

ELIZA. Cheaper than you'd get at the store and homemade tasty.

TIFFANY. Cracklin' good.

ELIZA. *(shooing* **TIFFANY** *away)* These are my customers, Tiffy. Go over yonder to that other table.

(She points to the table occupied by the **OLDER COUPLE.** **TIFFANY** *goes over and speaks to its occupants, although we we won't be able to hear their exchange.* **ELIZA** *picks up where she left off with her own customers. Through the dialogue that follows,* **HENRY, CAL,** *and* **IDA** *will listen in, fascinated,* **HENRY** *scribbling away in his book.* **ELIZA** *redirects herself to the* **YOUNG MAN** *sitting in front of her.)*

So how 'bout you buy a bag of these lip smackin', down-home blue ribbon kettle-rinds for your purdy little girlfriend here?

MAN. She isn't my girlfriend. She's my wife.

ELIZA. *(friendly, conversational)* Ain't that nice? You two got yourself any young 'uns?

WOMAN. *(turning her back to* ELIZA*)* Just ignore her, Clyde, and she'll go away.

MAN. *(ignoring his wife instead)* We've got a boy and girl. They're in Kiddie-Land right now with their grandparents.

WOMAN. *(chastising her husband with horror)* Don't tell this lowlife carnie where our children are!

ELIZA. Excuse me, Lady. But I ain't no lowlife carnie. I'm an independent contractor, and I ain't gonna hurt your little beauties! All I aim to do in this here fairgrounds is sell my tasty and nutritious pork products.

WOMAN. *(turning suddenly back around)* Nutritious?! There's nothing nutritious about pork rinds! They're artery-clogging high cholesterol delivery devices, that's what they are. And as for quality control – I lay good money, missy, that you don't even know what the words mean. Two dollars buys a bag full of trichinosis, is my guess. Get those disgusting things away from me.

ELIZA. *(dispirited)* You don't have to be so – it's a good product me and my pa make, it is, and we change our kettle oil at least onct a week. Now they ain't for everybody, that's a fact, but you don't see *me* goin' around tearin' down everthing *I* see that *I* don't happen to like. And you wanna know why? 'Cuz it just ain't polite!

MAN. *(gently, to* ELIZA*)* Maybe you better go.

ELIZA. I'll go. 'Cuz I got good manners. I'm a good girl, I am. 'Course, I cain't say the same for *you* –

(to the woman, who again turns her back to ELIZA*)*

And they are *so* nutritious. They got no – no –

TIFFANY. *(calling over, helpfully)* Carbohydrates! They got no carbohydrates!

*(*TIFFANY *is completing a successful transaction; she has just sold two bags of pork rinds.* ELIZA *is set to walk away when she sees* HENRY *jotting something in his notebook.)*

ELIZA. *(to* **HENRY***)* You fixin' to give me a ticket?

HENRY. A what?

ELIZA. *(nodding)* A ticket. For vendin' without I got a license.

HENRY. No.

ELIZA. Good, 'cuz I got three tickets today already and I don't need no more.

HENRY. Rest assured: I wasn't writing you a citation.

ELIZA. Then what *was* you writin' up in that there book?

HENRY. I was taking down what you were saying.

(He shows her the page on which he's been writing.)

ELIZA. That don't look like no language I ever seen before.

HENRY. That's because I'm writing phonetically.

ELIZA. Phone-what?

HENRY. *(reading from the notebook in Eliza's voice)* "I'm a good girl I am. 'Course I cain't say the same for *you.*"

ELIZA. Why are you writin' down the way I say things?

CAL. *(answering for his friend)* Because it's what he does. He teaches phonetic linguistics. He studies dialects.

ELIZA. Dia—what?

IDA. The way people talk, honey.

ELIZA. What is it about the way I talk, you gotta put it down on paper?

HENRY. I happen to *like* the way you talk. I happen to like the way a lot of people talk. It fascinates me. Now, take this nice woman here.

(indicating **IDA***)*

I have just told her, based upon her accent, where she was born and where she has lived. I did neglect, however, to make mention of her *present* address.

(turning to **IDA***)*

Wimpole Gardens would be my guess. Right here in town.

IDA. That's right!

(to **CAL***)*

Next he'll be telling me the very house I live in.

HENRY. The large Victorian with all the turrets at the corner of Warren and Candida.

IDA. You're dangerous!

HENRY. Simple deductive reasoning. I happen to know that this beautiful house has been in the Hill family for over 100 years. You said your name was Hill. I deduced.

IDA. *(giggling)* I'm going to start calling you Mr. Holmes.

(to **CAL***)*

Won't I, *Dr. Watson?*

*(***CAL*** *smiles.)*

ELIZA. I seen that house too. It's a right purdy house. Purdiest on the block.

IDA. Goodness. Now *everyone* knows where I live.

(indicating **ELIZA***)*

But what about the girl?

HENRY. Oh yes.

(consults his notebook)

Let me see: Yazoo Basin and a smattering of Bluff Hills, with a few months spent in the vicinity of Pontotoc Ridge.

ELIZA. *(noticeably impressed)* I got an aunt I used to spend summers with up in Tupelo. She learned me not to say "ain't," and then she died and I went back to talkin' the way I done talked before.

HENRY. Mississippi through and through.

*(***TIFFANY*** *has sauntered over now.)*

HENRY. *(still to* **ELIZA***:)* I'm going to guess you've hardly ever left the state.

ELIZA. Onct I went up to Memphis to have my ovaries looked at.

TIFFANY. But there warn't nothin' wrong with 'em. It was just this other aunt a'hearn, who got it into her addled brain that Eliza was fillin' up with eggs.

ELIZA. 'Cuz I liked to eat eggs. Tiffany's right. This aunt was a mite touched.

IDA. *(getting the names straight)* Eliza. Tiffany.

ELIZA. Eliza Doolittle. You know: Doolittle like that girl what sang so purdy on *American Idol?* This here is my friend Tiffany Box.

TIFFANY. *(shaking hands with everyone)* Pleased to meet you, Ms. –

IDA. Hill. Ida Hill. And this is Professor Henry Higgins. And over here we have Professor Calvin Pickering.

(They all shake hands. CAL seems more than a little interested in Tiffany.)

TIFFANY. *(snickering)* I knew a girl onct. Her name was Ida too. "Ida Better Not"!

(HENRY and IDA smile politely. CAL laughs effusively.)

CAL. "Ida Better Not." I like that.

ELIZA. *(to HENRY)* So you teach people how to talk?

HENRY. Well, I suppose I could give diction lessons if I chose to. But I've never really given it much thought.

ELIZA. My aunt in Tupelo didn't do a very good job. Or maybe I didn't do a very good job of learnin'. She'd make me sit with my mouth shut tight during her Wednesday night missionary circle meetings. She said them church ladies would find my voice to be an "offense unto God."

IDA. How horrible!

HENRY. She doesn't sound like a very nice aunt.

ELIZA. I reckon she did the best she could.

TIFFANY. She was a bitter old biddy, if you want the truth of it. You would have liked Eliza's uncle, though. He used to play in the dirt with Elvis back when them two was little sprouts. Eliza's aunt – why, she always thought her brother Cleeron was the one with the velvety voice. She thought her whole family got robbed by fate when it was Elvis who went and got hisself famous.

ELIZA. *(a gentle rebuke)* Tiffany, they don't wanna hear all that stuff about my family!

TIFFANY. I live here in town and Eliza lives with her pa on a pig farm a few miles south of town and none of us are famous, except some day I'm *gonna* be. Gonna go out on the stage. I got my stage name already – but Eliza here ain't gonna be nothin' but *poor* lessin' you buy some of her pork rinds.

ELIZA. That warn't a very nice way to put my sitchi-ation, Tiffany!

TIFFANY. *(confidentially to* ELIZA*)* Hush up! I was tryin' to get you a couple of pity-sales!

CAL. *(to* TIFFANY*)* A life on the stage, you say?

TIFFANY. *(with theatrical diffidence)* It's my dream.

ELIZA. I got a dream too. It ain't a big dream but it's a 'spectable one.

IDA. What would that be, honey?

ELIZA. I wanna get me a job as a waitress in one of them nice downtown barbecue places where all the tourists go. I could be good there 'cuz I know everything there is to know about hogs from piglet to plate, you know, on account of all my years of helpin' out my pa. Did you know that a pig is one of the smartest land mammals there is? Like even smarter than a dog or cat?

HENRY. I think I'd read something like that somewhere.

ELIZA. That's why it always pained me so much at slaughter time. If we could all drink pig milk 'stead of cow milk, then my pa wouldn't have to kill a single one of 'em and then I wouldn't have to be dryin' and smokin' their skins and puttin' 'em into bags like these – and Pa and me, we'd just open ourselves up a big ol' pig dairy farm. Pig milk. Pig cheese. Pig ice cream.

(**IDA** *appears suddenly queasy.*)

'Course ain't no good barbecue restaurant would hire the likes of me.

CAL. Why is that? You seem like a nice girl.

ELIZA. I *am* a nice girl. But people hear my voice and they don't think I'm a very *smart* girl.

IDA. Nonsense! We've been talking for less than ten minutes and I can already tell that you're just as bright as any other young woman your age. You just haven't had the educational opportunities that a lot of girls have had. Can you read, darling?

ELIZA. Yes ma'am. I taught myself to read all by myself after my pa pulled me out of school to help him with them pigs.

IDA. Now see there! That's an accomplishment.

TIFFANY. Liza's right though. She opens her mouth and Lord, it's like the hillbillies just loaded up their truck and moved to Bev-er-lee.

(to **HENRY***)*

Maybe, Professor, you could teach her a thing or two.

HENRY. Teach her?

TIFFANY. Like how to talk so it don't sound like she just fell off the watermelon truck.

HENRY. You mean lessons?

TIFFANY. Uh huh.

HENRY. *(shaking his head)* No, I wouldn't have time to give lessons.

CAL. Henry could make the time. But he won't.

IDA. *(to* **CAL***)* Now why do you say that?

CAL. How should I put this? Every stroll that Henry and I take through every Mississippi Delta town we visit – and we've visited just about every one of them – ends up with this one here pursing his lips and tutting like an old school marm and expounding ad infinitum on that same tired old subject: how a certain class of southerner has lost every last vestige of his affiliation with his native tongue.

TIFFANY. What's that you're sayin' in plain English?

CAL. That the rural southerner can't speak the language, or at least can't speak it in such a way as to be clearly understood and respected. The English language: it's the most sophisticated, the most complex, the most deliciously-nuanced language in the world – says he – but it's been largely abandoned by a sizeable segment of the American South.

ELIZA. *(hurt, to* **HENRY***)* Is that what you say? Is that what you say about people like Tiffany and me?

HENRY. *(to* **CAL***, angry)* Now why did you bring this up?

CAL. Because if you've said it once, you've said it a thousand times, Henry: give me one of these redneck, hillbilly, dirty-faced Dixieland ground-feeders and after six weeks, I could pass him off as the governor of Mississippi. But it isn't going to happen. Because most southerners are lazy. Why else do they drawl? Why else do their tongues just loll about in their mouths as if forced enunciation would put them into a coma for all the exertion?

HENRY. *(overlapping with* **ELIZA***)* That's enough, Cal.

ELIZA. *(overlapping, to* **HENRY***)* You say that? You talk about my people that way?

HENRY. *(a weak defense)* No. Not exactly.

(shooting daggers at **CAL***)*

Cal, I'm going to have you run over by a monster truck.

ELIZA. *(to* **HENRY***)* If that's the way you feel about us, then I'm sorry we even met. I thought you was all nice people.

TIFFANY. *(to* **HENRY***, with venom)* When you ain't nice at all! You're a cruel man, Professor Higgins, thinking that about people what ain't had the kind of good luck and fortune you've had. Cruel and mean and filled up to your eyeballs with shitty shit. And I bet you think your shit don't even stink!

ELIZA. Come on, Tiffany.

TIFFANY. *(on a roll)* Well, it *do*! And you wanna know *why*, Mr. Professor Man? 'Cuz of what you been eatin'. You been eatin' Uppity Stew is what you been eatin', Mr. Professor Man! Bowls and bowls of Uppity Stew!

*(***ELIZA*** starts to drag* **TIFFANY** *away. She stops and turns back to* **IDA***.)*

ELIZA. It was a pleasure to meet you, Ms. Hill.

(She wheels back around and the two storm off. There is a silence.)

HENRY. *(to* **CAL,** *with bitter sarcasm)* Thank you, Professor Pickering, for reminding me what an arrogant, class-conscious ass I am. Sometimes I forget. Oh yes, and for facilitating that lovely excursion into the bleak landscape of class animosity. How often does one get taken to task for dining on "Uppity Stew"?

CAL. I'm sorry, Henry. I didn't realize that they would take it so personally.

(gazing off in the direction of Eliza and Tiffany's departure)

Especially Tiffany.

(rapturously)

Such a feisty firebrand! Such ferocious, unfettered fury!

HENRY. *(with a seething undertone)* You're alliterating again, Cal, and I'm about to strike you.

(turning to go)

I'm going somewhere to clear my head. I think I need some funnel cake.

(to **IDA,** *empty words)*

Ms. Hill, it was an absolute delight.

(He goes. **CAL** *and* **IDA** *stare at one another for a moment.)*

CAL. He could really do it, you know.

IDA. Do what?

CAL. Help that girl get rid of her comical back-woods accent. Maybe actually get her a job in one of those downtown barbecue restaurants she mentioned.

IDA. But it's all rather moot now, wouldn't you say?

*(**CAL** sighs and nods. Lights fade out.)*

Scene Two

(Ida Hill's back terrace. It is furnished with nice wrought-iron garden furniture. **IDA** *is sitting, reading a newspaper and sipping from a coffee cup. There are other newspapers stacked and spread about the table. There is also evidence of a just-finished breakfast in front of her. Ida's maid,* **OPAL**, *enters with an empty clear-away tray.)*

OPAL. Would you like me to take away those dirty breakfast dishes, Ms. Hill?

IDA. Thank you, Opal. Any sign of my kids?

OPAL. They just got here, ma'am. I just saw them getting out of Freddy's car.

IDA. Well, direct them out here if you would. And tell them they're an hour and half late, so I went ahead and had my breakfast without them.

OPAL. Yes ma'am.

*(***IDA** *gathers up a couple of the newspapers and gives them to Opal.)*

IDA. Hide these, please, Opal. I don't want my kids to know that I read them.

*(***OPAL** *glances at one of the newspapers.)*

OPAL. *(pointing to an item in paper)* How is that little boy doing – the one who was born with a dog brain?

IDA. Well, he isn't barking nearly as much. I'd say that represents an improvement, wouldn't you?

OPAL. *(nodding)* You don't believe all of that stuff, do you, Ms. Hill?

IDA. Of course not! Except maybe the overweight celebrity pictures. It just brightens my day a little, that's all. But don't let my children see them, Opal. I'll never hear the last of it. Vicki wants me put away as it is.

(picks up juice glass and quickly drains it)

And don't you dare tell Clara that I've started drinking the black cherry juice. I'll never hear the last of her "I told you so" either.

OPAL. I won't mention it.

(OPAL laughs and goes out. IDA picks up a "serious" newspaper and returns to her morning read. CLARA and FREDDY enter, accompanied by their sister VICKI. VICKI is a snoot; you can see it in her face and comportment the moment you meet her. All go to kiss their mother good morning.)

IDA. You're late.

FREDDY. Yes, we've already been informed.

(He pulls up a chair and sits casually astride it.)

CLARA. We had a meeting, Mama. Vicki was outvoted. We want to take you down to the Gulf – to where you and Daddy spent your honeymoon.

IDA. *(to VICKI)* What was *your* vote, honey?

VICKI. I voted for New York. It was a waste of vocal cords.

CLARA. Vicki doesn't mind people who live *beyond* their means, but she abhors those who choose to live *below* them.

VICKI. *(to CLARA)* Do you know what people call that awful stretch of beach where the two of you want to take Mother? It's called "The Redneck Riveria." This is your idea of a family vacation? Playing Skee-ball and slathering on cheap coconut suntan lotion and gorging yourself on crayfish like hungry swamp rats?

FREDDY. "Crawdads," sister. I think that's the proper local term. Get your characterizations straight. Anyway, I'm not invested in any particular place. I just want Mom to be happy.

(IDA smiles and blows her son a motherly kiss.)

VICKI. Which means if Mother says she'd like to go to New York, you'll change your vote to New York?

FREDDY. *(shrugging)* Sure. Why not?

CLARA. *(suddenly thrown into a panic)* But New York isn't where Mama and Daddy went for their honeymoon.

VICKI. Why would Mother want to go to the place where she spent her honeymoon? She had a horrible time there!

IDA. *(to* **CLARA***)* Vicki is right. I had a horrible time there.

(to **VICKI***)*

But your father was there and that made it all wonderful. Let's talk about something else.

*(***OPAL** *enters.)*

I've already cried over the memory of your father once this morning and I'd prefer not to do again.

OPAL. Ms. Hill – there's a young woman here to see you.

VICKI. *(to* **OPAL***)* Tell her to go away.

(to **IDA***)*

It's probably that homeless-looking woman we passed coming down the street.

IDA. *(to* **OPAL***)* Did she say what she wanted?

OPAL. Just that she'd like to talk to you. She said she'd spent the whole morning on the bus and she's hoping it wasn't for nothing.

IDA. Well, where in the world is this poor young woman coming from that she should have to spend an entire morning on a bus just to see *me?*

OPAL. Her father's pig farm she said.

*(***IDA** *makes the connection. Her eyes light up.)*

IDA. Send her out, Opal. Ask her if she's thirsty and send her right out here with something cool to drink.

*(***OPAL** *nods and exits.)*

VICKI. *Pig farm?*

IDA. Didn't I tell you about the two young women I met at the fair?

VICKI. No you did not.

FREDDY. *(to* **VICKI***, indicating* **CLARA** *and himself)* She told *us.* The girl sounds interesting.

VICKI. *(to* **IDA***)* How did she find out where you live?

IDA. Well, it just came out in the conversation.

VICKI. Mother, are you *insane?*

CLARA. *(to* **VICKI***)* Don't call Mama insane, Vicki.

VICKI. I'll call her whatever she deserves. Ever since Daddy died she –

(directing herself to **IDA***)*

You've been different. I don't like it, Mother. I don't like the way you've changed. Daddy wouldn't have liked it either.

IDA. *(disagreeing)* Your father started out as a public defender, honey – a man of the people. *And* he ate pork rinds.

(to **CLARA** *and* **FREDDY***)*

I forgot to tell Eliza that. I forgot to tell her that my late husband had a secret passion for fried pork skins.

*(***ELIZA** *comes out, carrying a glass with a pink liquid inside. She has overheard this last line.* **FREDDY** *turns around and seeing Eliza, jumps to his feet, instantly taken with her.)*

ELIZA. *(genially)* Now that would've been a right nice thing to know!

IDA. I meant to tell you. And I was meaning to buy some of your pork rinds too. But you left in such a hurry.

*(***FREDDY** *offers his hand to shake.* **ELIZA** *takes it.)*

FREDDY. I'm Freddy.

IDA. *(making introductions)* This is Eliza, Freddy. Eliza Doolittle. Eliza, these are my three children. That's Clara there.

(The two shake.)

And the one wearing the scowl would be Vicki, my youngest.

*(***ELIZA** *extends her hand to shake Vicki's, but* **VICKI** *doesn't condescend to take it.)*

ELIZA. *(with down-home politeness)* I'm pleased to know you all.

CLARA. Mama tells us you met at the fair.

*(***ELIZA*** *nods.)*

IDA. *(genuine interest, to* **ELIZA***)* Did you sell all your wares, honey?

ELIZA. No ma'am. I didn't do as good as Tiffany. But I'll do better tonight. The last night of the fair, folks is usually purdy hungry.

IDA. And where is your friend Tiffany right now?

ELIZA. Sawin' logs more than likely. Tiffy keeps them late hours, don't cha know? She goes to them clubs and dances and spins herself dizzy till two or three in the morning some nights.

IDA. You wanted to see me, Eliza?

ELIZA. Yes ma'am. If'n I ain't interrupting nothin'.

IDA. May I have a few minutes with Ms. Doolittle, children? Why don't you go in and see what Genevieve's making for lunch?

*(***FREDDY***,* **VICKI** *and* **CLARA** *start inside.* **FREDDY** *is unable to take his eyes off Eliza. He is clearly enamored.* **VICKI** *stops and turns back to address her mother.)*

VICKI. What happened to Dorothy? I used to love the lunches that Dorothy made.

IDA. Dorothy doesn't work here anymore, honey. You accused her of stealing.

VICKI. *(remembering)* That's right. And she *was* stealing!

IDA. Fiddlesticks! She took home only what I gave her. You jumped to unfortunate conclusions about the cook, dear.

(to **ELIZA***, with mock confidentiality)*

She does that: she jumps to conclusions about people. I don't know what to do with her.

CLARA. *(overhearing)* Disown her.

(On **VICKI***'s appalled reaction, Ida's three offspring exit.)*

IDA. *(to* **ELIZA***)* Sit. Drink your lemonade. Is it good? Opal said you've been riding a bus all morning.

ELIZA. *Three* buses. Two connections.

IDA. I hope it wasn't too tiring for you to get here.

ELIZA. It would have been if Pa hadn't said he'd slop the hogs for me. Sometimes Pa'll do my chores when I got things in the city I gotta do.

IDA. Your father sounds like a good man.

ELIZA. He *is* a good man. Mostly. He drinks a little too much but he ain't a mean drunk – just a sleepy drunk.

IDA. Perhaps I'll have the pleasure of meeting him some day.

ELIZA. I think he'd like you.

(getting to what she came to say)

Ms. Hill?

IDA. Yes, what is it, Eliza?

ELIZA. Remember what that Professor Pickering said about Professor Higgins?

IDA. Well, he said a lot of things, honey. What specifically would you like me to remember?

ELIZA. About him being able to teach people how not to talk the way I'm talkin' right now.

IDA. Yes, I recall that.

ELIZA. Do you think it's true?

IDA. I don't know why it wouldn't be. Mr. Higgins is a not-untalented man – we saw that for ourselves.

ELIZA. Do you think he might want to teach *me?* If'n he knew I was really serious about takin' the lessons.

IDA. Well, dear, I don't know him well enough to know whether he'd want to teach you or not.

ELIZA. Could you maybe talk to him for me?

IDA. Talk to him?

ELIZA. Yes ma'am – put in a good word for me.

IDA. Don't you think it would be better for you to talk to him yourself? There were harsh words exchanged between the two of you if I recall. Shouldn't all of that be ironed out first?

ELIZA. You could be the one to iron it out. Oh Ms. Hill, I wouldn't know what to say to him after the way Tiffany reamed him out six ways to Sunday – and 'specially after how my face looked when his friend said them things to begin with. Like somebody done hit me with a two-ba.

IDA. A tuba?

(with large gestures)

You mean like a big, you know – "oompa oompa"?

ELIZA. No ma'am. A two-ba like a two-ba-four.

IDA. Oh I see.

(seriously contemplating Eliza's request)

So you'd like for me to smooth it all over for you?

ELIZA. *(nodding)* And then ask him all polite-like if he could teach me to talk like somebody what could work in a nice barbecue restaurant. I could pay him. I ain't indigenous.

IDA. "Indigenous"? Oh, you must mean "indigent."

ELIZA. Yes ma'am. I get money from the work I do for my pa and from sellin' my pork rinds. I could pay for lessons.

IDA. *(after a moment's thought and without too much reluctance)* All right. I'll do it.

ELIZA. Oh thank you, ma'am. Thank you so much!

(She throws her arms around IDA, who accepts the hug without too much discomfort.)

IDA. Now when would you like me to speak with the good Professor?

ELIZA. Right now.

IDA. This very moment?

(ELIZA nods.)

But honey, I don't even know where he is right now.

ELIZA. He's at the college. I called him up on the pay phone and the operator lady put me through to his office. I'm purdy sure it was him who said hello, but I didn't say nothin' 'cuz I wanted to talk to you first. But it don't make no never mind. You're either gonna find him in his office or in his classroom, I'll betcha.

IDA. Goodness. I hadn't thought about going out today. The pool-boy is coming to close up the swimming pool for the season.

ELIZA. Do you got to watch the pool-boy do his work?

IDA. I suppose I don't *have* to. But you see, he looks a little like my late husband, when he was young, you understand.

ELIZA. Cain't you look at the pool-boy some other day?

IDA. *(this settles it)* Certainly.

(She gets up. ELIZA rises with her.)

I can always call him back here for some reason or another. I know: I'll tell him that raccoons knocked over the tub of chlorine tablets again. I haven't used that one in a while.

(ELIZA smiles.)

Now you sit right here while I go and get dressed. Then we'll drive over to the college and I'll put in my good word for you while you wait out in the car. After that, I'm taking you right back down to your father's farm – three buses in one day is three buses too many for anyone.

ELIZA. *(remonstrating)* Now you ain't drivin' all that way on my account.

IDA. Of course I am.

ELIZA. But I gotta work the fair tonight.

IDA. I don't see your pork rinds.

ELIZA. I always leave 'em at Tiffany's house here in town.

IDA. Then I'll buy all the bags you were planning on peddling tonight.

ELIZA. But you cain't buy 'em all. There are pert near fifty bags over there!

IDA. I'm buying all your pork rinds, Eliza, and that's settled.

ELIZA. *(with a smile)* Golly Molly! I come to your house to ask you a favor and you do me *two* favors and give me this here tasty lemonade on top of it all!

IDA. It's because I like you, Eliza.

*(**IDA** pinches Eliza's nose with affection, then goes off. For the next few moments, **ELIZA** is left alone with her thoughts. She paces a little, examines plantings, takes the fresh morning air into her lungs. **FREDDY** comes out of the house. He stands for a moment looking at her – admiring her. Finally she notices him with a start.)*

FREDDY. I'm sorry. I didn't mean to scare you.

ELIZA. For a second I thought you was the pool-boy.

FREDDY. Do I look like a "pool-boy"?

ELIZA. Your ma was talking about him.

FREDDY. *(nodding)* Apparently Mom has taken a special interest in him. In spite of the fact that he's at least thirty years her junior, and we all suspect that he's – how shall I put this? – *gay.*

ELIZA. Oh.

(after a beat)

Are *you* gay?

FREDDY. Do I appear gay to you?

ELIZA. I suppose not. 'Course all the homosexuals *I* know wear overalls and work on their trucks, so I cain't be the one to say. I used to think my friend Tiffany was gay. But it turns out he ain't gay at all. He's just a woman. I mean – inside. Outside too, if you don't look too close. Why are *you* looking at *me* that way?

FREDDY. I'm sorry. I find you fascinating. I've never met a pig farmer's daughter before.

ELIZA. Well, then take a long gander 'cuz I don't aim to be one for much longer – I mean, I guess I'll always be the daughter of a pig farmer so long as Pa keeps the farm, but I don't aim to be on that farm any longer than I gotta be.

FREDDY. Does this have anything to do with my mother?

ELIZA. *(nodding)* She's gonna talk to Professor Higgins for me. She's gonna ask him to teach me how to talk.

FREDDY. *I'm* having no trouble understanding you.

ELIZA. That ain't it.

FREDDY. No, no, I get your meaning. It's about more than just being understood, isn't it?

(**ELIZA** *nods.*)

Soooo…

(**FREDDY** *takes a breath.*)

…would you like to go out with me?

ELIZA. Go – ?

FREDDY. Out.

ELIZA. Where?

FREDDY. Maybe see a movie or something. Grab some dinner.

ELIZA. Like when?

FREDDY. How about tonight?

ELIZA. I don't rightly –

FREDDY. Pa expecting you back at an early hour?

ELIZA. No, that ain't it.

FREDDY. Do I turn you off? I've been known to turn some women off. Especially friends of Vicki's. I'm – how did they describe me – *uncouth.*

ELIZA. You seem purdy couth to me I reckon.

FREDDY. Okay, okay. I'm rushing things. I do that.

(*He takes a step back.*)

I'm backing off a little, see? I'm biding my time. I'm a patient man.

(ELIZA smiles.)

ELIZA. You're also a very nice man. As nice as your ma. I didn't know that rich people could be so nice.

FREDDY. And just how many rich people do you know?

ELIZA. Not many, I reckon.

FREDDY. You're almost out of lemonade. Let me get you a refill.

(He snatches the glass from her hand.)

Vicki says its gauche to drink lemonade after Labor Day. Vicki says a lot of things we don't pay much attention to. Sit down. I'll be right back.

(He goes into the house. ELIZA sits down. A moment later, CLARA comes out. She pulls up a chair and sits down next to ELIZA. She folds her hands in her lap and stares into the middle distance, lost in a reverie. She comes out of it, turns to ELIZA and notices her staring.)

CLARA. *(explaining herself)* I'm waiting for Gerald.

ELIZA. Who's Gerald?

CLARA. He's the pool-boy.

ELIZA. Your brother says he's a homosexual man.

CLARA. Doesn't stop a person from looking.

(indicating where ELIZA is sitting)

You've picked a good seat, by the way. Unobstructed view.

(Stage goes black.)

Scene Three

(Henry Higgins' classroom, represented by a blackboard, a large teacher's desk and several student desks. **HENRY** *is alone. He is putting the following words on the black-board: "through, enough, thorough, bough, cough, hiccough."* **IDA** *pokes her head into the classroom.)*

IDA. Hello?

*(***HENRY** *turns to her. Recognizing her instantly, he smiles and goes to her.)*

HENRY. Hello – Ms. Hill was it?

(They shake hands.)

IDA. Yes but call me Ida.

HENRY. Henry will do for me. What brings you to Covent College this afternoon?

IDA. To see you.

HENRY. I'm flattered. I enjoyed making your acquaintance at the fairgrounds on Tuesday.

IDA. As did I you.

HENRY. "A most interesting time was had by all."

IDA. Yes it was quite interesting. Henry, your friend Professor Pickering – *Cal* – mentioned something about the theoretical possibility of your giving diction lessons.

HENRY. He did.

(beat, then with a shrug)

Although, I've never given diction lessons before.

IDA. And that's why I used the word "theoretical." I'm mindful that I'm in a college setting, so I am attempting to use collegiate words.

HENRY. *(playfully)* Collegiate *and* collegial. I commend you.

IDA. But you could do it. The lessons, I mean.

HENRY. I'm certain that I could.

IDA. If you weren't too busy.

HENRY. Your diction doesn't seem wanting of correction to *my* ear, Ida.

IDA. I wasn't asking for myself.

(**HENRY** *stares at* **IDA,** *not understanding.*)

They'd be for that young woman we met the other night. Eliza.

HENRY. The daughter of the pig farmer. The one selling the homemade pork rinds?

IDA. That's right. She came to see me this morning. She had to take three buses.

HENRY. I beg your pardon?

IDA. She's quite desperate for lessons, Henry – so she can work in one of those tourist restaurants downtown. She seems very deserving to me. I mean, if you could make the time.

HENRY. There are other people, specifically trained for this purpose. They could just as easily drain the "redneck" from her speech.

IDA. But Eliza seems determined to have *you.* It's all she talked about in the car coming over here.

HENRY. She's *here?*

IDA. Right down the hall. She didn't want to wait in the car. I left her in the student lounge.

HENRY. *(half to himself)* Calvin's the cause of all this. He's the one who wanted to play the "game." I would have been content to make my notes in private and keep all my surmises to myself.

IDA. Well, now the damage has been done, and there's a young, very earnest pig farmer's daughter out there who no longer *wishes* to talk like a pig farmer's daughter, and she wants *you* to be the one to give her lessons. And I do too. In fact, I absolutely *dare* you to do it.

(with playful, transparent insincerity)

Because I, frankly, don't think you can pull it off. So you'll have to prove me wrong. You'll have to prove to me that you are fully capable of providing this sweet girl with a respectable suburban middle class southern accent within six weeks, or I'll be forced to go all over town and tell everyone I meet what a terrible fraud you are.

HENRY. *(with a grin)* And this respectable suburban middle class southern accent of which you speak – would that make Aunt *(pronounced "Ain't" like Opie's "Aint Bee")* Louise an *Aunt (rhymes with "taunt")* or an *Aunt ("ant")*?

IDA. Oh, I don't want the girl to put on airs; a simple "ant" will do.

HENRY. Of course, if she were Bostonian or African-American, "Aunt" *(rhymes with "taunt")* would not only be acceptable but preferred and by no means looked upon as "putting on airs."

IDA. Yes, yes, you're so right, Henry. You're a whiz at this whole phonetics and accents business, which is why you really should be the one to help the girl.

HENRY. What about your dare?

IDA. Forget the dare. I'm sure that you saw right through it.

HENRY. All right. I'll think about it. I'm frankly amazed that Eliza would even want me as her teacher after Calvin made me out to be such a contemptible, class-conscious buffoon.

IDA. I think she'd have you in spite of your potential buffoonery, Henry. She's very earnest, as I might have mentioned.

HENRY. In spite of my –? So do *you* think I'm the way that Calvin described me?

IDA. I not only think it, Henry, I *know* it. I did a little googling of you and your colleague after I got home from the fair the other night, and discovered to my delight and surprise that the two of you aren't the patched-tweed, all-but-pauperish college professors you purport to be, but actually two of the richest men in the state of Mississippi. If you think you've been keeping this tidy little secret all to yourselves, think again.

HENRY. *(a side regret)* I really need to google myself more often.

IDA. I'm sure that the administrators of this college have been on to you for some time.

HENRY. All the better. This just proves that they keep Calvin and me around not because of *whom* we are but because of what we do – what we are *good* at.

IDA. Which brings us full circle, Henry. You are very good at what you do and you should use that gift to help Eliza. And if you don't, I will trade on all the good will that has been built up for my late husband as one of the most beloved trustees of this college, and put polite but firm pressure on this institution to instruct its development people to hound you every day of your remaining tenure for a large and generous endowment from your vast stores of family wealth.

HENRY. Ida. You do not have to blackmail me into teaching the girl. I had just a moment ago decided to do it anyway. If only to show her that I wasn't the class-conscious snob she believes me to be. Now, how I might go about proving this to *you*, well, that's another matter altogether.

IDA. Do this for the girl, Henry, and I promise to hold you in only the highest, warmest regard. Shall I bring her in?

HENRY. I have a class in an hour.

IDA. That's long enough for a first lesson. I'll busy myself by making friends with all the good folk in the Covent College Development Office.

HENRY. I will have you know that Calvin and I do not sit on our money. We put a great deal of it to work in various charitable causes.

IDA. Name one.

HENRY. I am a big supporter of the Shawsville Anthropological Museum, if you must know. So is Calvin. The museum represents a nice intersection of our interests.

IDA. You support a museum *about* people, but do you actually support *people?* My husband did. I'll fetch Eliza.

(**IDA** *goes. A moment passes. Now* **CAL** *pokes his head into the room.*)

CAL. That was harsh.

HENRY. How long have you been eavesdropping?

CAL. I think I started listening in at "hello."

HENRY. What do you want?

CAL. Just a phone number. Of the other one – the one who calls herself Tiffany.

HENRY. You want me to ask Eliza for Tiffany's number?

CAL. Yes. That's what I just said.

HENRY. And why?

CAL. I want to get to know her better.

HENRY. *(dryly)* Of course you do.

CAL. Don't judge my tastes, Henry. There's a lot more black on your kettle than my pot.

HENRY. What the hell is that supposed to mean?

CAL. It means that you have your own quirks, Henry. Some which could be judged good, some which could be judged suspect. According to Ms. Hill, for example, you do not help people. You really should start helping people.

HENRY. Like you're going to help Tiffany Box. Ida Hill should know exactly how you plan on helping Tiffany Box.

CAL. *(sincerely offended)* I rebuke the lechery implied by that remark!

HENRY. Rebuke away on your own time, Cal. I've got a student on the way.

CAL. *(suddenly contrite)* Forgive the snipe. Just get me Tiffany's phone number. The only "Box" I could get from directory assistance is a cardboard packaging company.

(beat)

I haven't stopped thinking about her, Henry.

(He goes.)

HENRY. But she isn't even a...

(the volume of his voice dropping impotently)

...*woman.*

(**HENRY** *sighs and sits down behind his desk. A moment later* **ELIZA** *enters.* **HENRY** *rises to greet her.*)

HENRY. *(cont.)* Hello, Ms. Doolitte – *Eliza.*

ELIZA. *(taking his hand and pumping it gratefully)* Thank you so much for giving me lessons. I can pay you whatever you think is fair.

HENRY. I don't need your money, Eliza.

ELIZA. But I *have* to pay you. I don't give my pork rinds away for free and you shouldn't be giving lessons to people not without they pay *you.*

HENRY. Then we'll work something out.

(**ELIZA** *notices the words on the blackboard.*)

ELIZA. What's *that?*

HENRY. What's what?

ELIZA. Them words.

HENRY. *(gently correcting) Those* words. What do you *think* they are?

ELIZA. A bunch of – well – *words.*

HENRY. But do you notice anything they might have in common?

ELIZA. *(peering intently at the words on the board)* They have some of the same letters: "o-u-g-h."

HENRY. And what's unique about each one?

(**ELIZA** *shrugs.*)

Say them.

ELIZA. Through. Enough. Thorough. Bough. Cough. Hic-coff.

HENRY. *(correcting)* Hiccough. *(pronounced like "hiccup")* It's an alternative spelling.

ELIZA. All them words have a different sound.

HENRY. All of *those* words.

ELIZA. Why?

HENRY. Why what?

ELIZA. Why do they have different sounds when they all have o-u-g-h in 'em?

HENRY. Well, that's the point I was going to make to my linguistics class. I wanted to use those words to demonstrate the idiosyncratic nature of our language through the idiosyncrasies of our variant spellings.

ELIZA. The idio what?

HENRY. The English language has far too many rules and then far too many exceptions to those far-too-many-rules, and that's why it fascinates me immensely. How such a historically jerry-rigged, higgledy-piggledy language could even have developed, let alone achieved preeminence among all the languages of the world – it's really quite an achievement, wouldn't you say?

ELIZA. Do you like teaching this language stuff?

HENRY. I really do, Eliza. It's why I get up in the morning.

ELIZA. There ain't no other reason you get up in the mornin'?

HENRY. Well, of course there are other – I suppose I was just being hyper – *Aren't.* Not ain't. *Aren't* any other reasons to get up in the morning, even though there are. Didn't you say your aunt taught you to stop saying "ain't"?

ELIZA. She did.

HENRY. Then why did you go back?

ELIZA. 'Cuz she warn't riding herd on me no more.

HENRY. Any more.

ELIZA. Any more. Besides, it felt funny sayin' "aren't" and the other one –

HENRY. *(helping her)* "Isn't"

ELIZA. Yep. It felt funny talkin' that way in front of my pa and in front of my friends so I just kinda fell back into it. 'Cuz I didn't want them to think that I thought I was better than them.

HENRY. But aren't you up against the same thing now?

ELIZA. *(shaking her head)* Now I don't care so much what they think. 'Cuz I've decided I don't want to spend the rest of my life sloppin' hogs. I want somethin' more. Has our first lesson started?

HENRY. I suppose.

ELIZA. But I ain't – *aren't – isn't –*

HENRY. Am not.

ELIZA. Am not sitting in one of them –

HENRY. Those.

ELIZA. Those desks. *(pronounced "dess")*

HENRY. Desks.

ELIZA. That's what I said.

HENRY. No, Eliza. You said, "dess." It's a common southern pronunciation. But you should learn to say some words without all the molasses.

ELIZA. Molasses?

HENRY. The drawl and the slide. "Desks." Hear the k.

ELIZA. Dess.

HENRY. Desks.

ELIZA. Dess.

HENRY. Try to slip the "k" in there.

ELIZA. My mouth don't want the "k." It makes my mouth tired.

HENRY. Then you need to exercise your mouth a little more.

ELIZA. Desksksks.

HENRY. That's better.

ELIZA. Has the lesson started? I'm not sitting down.

HENRY. Then sit down.

(beat)

And you didn't say "ain't." Gold star for you.

*(**ELIZA** goes and sits down in one of the student desks. She takes out a small notebook and pen. She is ready. **HENRY** is not so ready.)*

Well. Okay.

(He gets up and takes a thoughtful stride or two across the room.)

HENRY. *(cont.)* I suppose I should start off by saying –

(**ELIZA** *is busy scribbling on her pad.*)

What are you doing?

ELIZA. *("What do you think I'm doing?")* I'm taking notes.

HENRY. But I haven't said anything yet.

ELIZA. Yes you have. You said:

(She reads:)

"I suppose I should start off by saying –"

HENRY. You're going to write down everything I say?

ELIZA. Isn't I supposed to?

HENRY. Why of course not.

ELIZA. Then how am I gonna learn nothin'? I ain't – aren't – stupid but you don't 'spect me to sit here and you learn me all this diction stuff not without I got some way to pin it all to my brain. 'Ain't – aren't – gonna happen no other way, no how.

HENRY. Eliza, there were about fifteen things wrong with what you just said, the first of course being that you *don't* have to write down everything I say. We'll be visiting certain areas over and over again and you'll absorb it all largely by rote.

ELIZA. But I done "rote" it and you told me not to.

HENRY. That's not the kind of "rote" I'm talking about.

ELIZA. Then what in fire and tarnation are you talkin' about?

HENRY. Eliza, there is no such word as "tarnation."

ELIZA. There is so. My Uncle Cleeron used to say it all the time: "fire and tarnation." 'Cuz he couldn't say "damnation" or my aunt would put the broom to his hind side.

HENRY. *(nodding – he's actually learning something himself)* Tarnation. Euphemism for "damnation." Yes, I understand. But could we start to divest ourselves of the more blatantly colloquial of your exclamatory interjections?

ELIZA. The what?

HENRY. The kind of verbal ejaculations –

(quickly correcting himself)

Phrases. Words and phrases that put you smack dab on the wrong side of the class divide.

ELIZA. *(grinning)* You said "smack dab."

HENRY. I did? So I did. What of it?

ELIZA. My father says "smack dab" and he's a pig farmer. You said it and you're a college professor. How do I aim to learn nothin' different if you're sayin' the same blamed things my pa's sayin'?

HENRY. Well, this, then, is a good place for us to talk about acceptable southern vernacular and *un*acceptable southern vernacular.

ELIZA. You mean there are certain ways of talkin' that might sound funny to a Yankee but don't sound so bad to folks down here?

HENRY. That's one way of looking at it.

ELIZA. So if you said "smack dab" in front of somebody from up north they might think you was stupid or something?

HENRY. Well, maybe. I don't know. That's their problem.

ELIZA. Then why would you say it?

HENRY. I just told you, Eliza – because it's part of acceptable southern vernacular speech.

ELIZA. Even if a Yankee thinks you're stupid like the same way you think *I'm* stupid?

HENRY. For crying out loud, Eliza, I don't think you're stupid.

ELIZA. But I *sound* stupid, else'n I woulda got hired at one of them restaurants I applied at.

HENRY. So you've already applied once at these places and they turned you down?

*(**ELIZA** nods despondently.)*

I'm sorry you had to go through that.

ELIZA. It warn't nothin' new. I tried to apply for a job as one of them telephone answerers at a mail order company here in town and the lady what did the hiring just laughed at me.

HENRY. *(correcting)* The lady *who* did the hiring. The personnel manager.

(ELIZA nods.)

Well, that's something that I aim to – rather, that I *intend* to fix.

ELIZA. So you really think you can help me?

HENRY. I do. Did you have doubts?

ELIZA. No. I dunno. Tiffany said you can take the girl out of the redneck but you cain't take the redneck out of the girl. But she was drunk at the time, and Tiffany don't hardly know what she's sayin' half the time any way. By the way: she's sorry for what she said to you the other night, Henry – you know: blowin' her stack like that. She's real sorry.

HENRY. Cal shouldn't have opened that door.

ELIZA. Do you really think you're better than some people?

HENRY. On occasion. But not in the way that you might think.

ELIZA. I don't get your meaning.

HENRY. What I mean is that I don't, as a rule, feel that I'm better – or even have the *right* to feel superior to anyone. With one exception. I don't have much tolerance for people who glide through life without making any effort to improve themselves. There is always room for us to pull ourselves up and try to make some kind of difference in this world. Too many people don't. Too many people are content just to sit and watch the parade go by.

ELIZA. I've watched a parade or two myself.

HENRY. But you don't sit on the sidelines as a rule. I've learned that much about you, Eliza. And I respect you for that. I respect you for coming here today. For going to see Ida this morning. That took a lot of courage.

ELIZA. It warn't nothin'.

HENRY. Well –

ELIZA. And by the way: I wouldn't of been watchin' them two parades if'n Tiffany hadn't been in 'em. They was those special parades that gay people put on. Tiffany wore fruit on her head in the last one. She thinks it was the watermelon what gave her the headache.

HENRY. What did your friend Tiffany say about my friend Cal? Was she just as upset with him as she was with me?

ELIZA. *(shaking her head)* Not atall. She actually cottoned to him purdy good.

HENRY. She did?

ELIZA. Couldn't stop talkin' about what a handsome older man he was.

HENRY. *Older* man? Older like *me?*

ELIZA. Yep. But neither of ya'll are old in my book. Land-sakes, my pa was a fifty-year-old man the day I was born. Now Pa is old, I'd say. Ain't slowed him down too much but he's still old in anybody's book. You'd be a shoat next to him.

HENRY. *(with a smile)* A shoat?

ELIZA. A real young pig.

HENRY. *(still smiling)* We should probably get to work. I've got a class coming in here soon.

ELIZA. How 'bout you *tell* me what I oughter be writin' down?

HENRY. That sounds like a good plan.

(He turns and goes to the board.)

ELIZA. Henry?

(He turns around.)

Thank you.

HENRY. Think nothing of it.

(He starts to write: "Ain't," then a dash, then "Aren't" as lights slowly fade out. End of Act One.)

ACT TWO

Scene One

(Lights come up on Tiffany's apartment. It is a small studio [or "efficiency" as it's sometimes called in southern cities]. The apartment can be most economically suggested by a couch and chair to one side, and a small dining room table on the other. It is at the dining room table that **TIFFANY** *has seated herself and is finishing a sandwich. She gets up and goes to an implied door.)*

TIFFANY. *(calling offstage)* How long does it take to put on a pantsuit? What are you doin' in there?

ELIZA'S VOICE. *(from offstage)* I feel funny.

TIFFANY. You'll be gorgeous. Get your butt out here so I can see you in the good light.

ELIZA'S VOICE. I will. I will.

(Tiffany's cell phone rings. She goes to where it lies on the couch, picks it up, and pops it open.)

TIFFANY. *(into phone)* Hello?

ELIZA'S VOICE. Who is it?

TIFFANY. *(into phone)* Hi Clara.

(calling to **ELIZA***)*

It's your friend Clara – Ida's daughter.

(listens)

Yeah, she's here. But I don't think she can come to the phone right now. She's in the middle of a fashion emergency. I mean she *thinks* it's an emergency – bless her heart – but it ain't really.

(listens)

TIFFANY. *(cont.)* Why, I gave her a total makeover, baby! For her first date with your brother. She's scared as hell but she's gonna do just fine. You want that I should have her call you when she comes out her little hidey hole?

(listens)

I sure will, sugar. Bye now.

(She hangs up. Calls into the back bedroom again.)

Eliza Doolittle, if you don't get yourself out here this minute, I'm gonna come in there and drag you out caveman-style. Dreamboy's gonna be here any minute now and I gotta make my last minute adjustments to your "toilette."

(Slowly and hesitatingly, ELIZA emerges. She has been transformed by her drag queen friend TIFFANY into a hooker-clown. Her face is made-up in garish colors. She wears too-high heels and her sequined pant suit looks as if it belongs to a low-rent homemaker on the prowl for extramarital adventure. Poor ELIZA is a caricature of a voluptuous woman, and TIFFANY doesn't perceive the cartoon; she is nothing if not pleased with the result. But remember that Tiffany is also a drag queen.)

TIFFANY. Ooh, honey. Let me look at you. Turn around. I could eat you up.

(ELIZA, in turning around, nearly topples off her shoes. She isn't used to the heels – especially ones this high.)

ELIZA. I dunno, Tiffy.

TIFFANY. Don't know what, darlin'? You could charm the husk right off of the corn!

ELIZA. I ain't never worn so much makeup in all my life.

TIFFANY. You never had a rich boyfriend neither.

ELIZA. He ain't my boyfriend.

TIFFANY. Well, he's certainly *gonna* be after tonight.

ELIZA. You don't think I might scare him away in all this get-up?

TIFFANY. Scare him away!? Honey, by night's end, you're gonna have him eatin' out of your hand. Listen to me, sugar – I know what the mens like.

ELIZA. Maybe I don't *want* to have him eating out of my hand, Tiffany. It took me two weeks just to get up the courage to go out with him.

TIFFANY. You're just shy, that's all.

ELIZA. No, it ain't that – I mean, not all of it.

(She sits down on the couch. TIFFANY *comes around behind her and makes some adjustments to Eliza's poofy hairdo.)*

TIFFANY. Then what is it, sugar? Some girls would kill to have a nice-lookin' man like Freddy Hill chasin' after 'em.

ELIZA. I wanted to wait till Professor Higgins had changed me up a little more. But it's been two weeks now of lessons every single day and I ain't hardly changed at all. I ain't even stopped usin' the word "ain't," for cryin' out loud.

TIFFANY. Maybe it's gonna take a little more time than you and the Professor was figurin'.

ELIZA. Or *maybe* –

(fearfully)

Or maybe I cain't be taught. Maybe there ain't nothin' can be done with me, and maybe I oughter just go back to them pigs and quit wastin' everybody's time.

TIFFANY. Eliza Jane Doolittle – you take that silly thought right out of your head. Don't do nobody good to be thinkin' that way. And besides, let's us say that worse comes to worst, baby, and the Professor ain't able to do nothin' for you –

ELIZA. See, I knew you was changin' your mind about all this too.

TIFFANY. No, I'm just sayin', sugarpie, if'n it don't happen. *If.* Why, it ain't the fine, cultured, nice-talkin' Eliza Doolittle that Freddy Hill's done fell in love with. It's the pig farmer's daughter, the pork-rind seller, the purdy country girl with the purdy country-girl smile – why, that's the one he wants to spend time with.

ELIZA. But I think he liked it that I wanted to improve myself. I think he liked that-there part of me more than anything else.

TIFFANY. Well, you still want to improve yourself, baby. The wantin's still there. It's just that not everybody gets to get what they want.

ELIZA. See? You *have* given up on me.

TIFFANY. I ain't givin' up on you, peanut. I'm just sayin' if it don't happen, why, you gotta be glad for the things that you want out of life that you *do* get to have. Now Freddy – he don't care how you talk. He loves you for *you.* And what you got goin' on the inside's gonna be there whether you talk like a Higgins or a Hill or a country farm girl named Doolittle. It's all the same.

ELIZA. Then why ain't *you* Roger Bosco – instead of some girly girl named Tiffany Box?

TIFFANY. That's a horse of a different hue, m'dear.

ELIZA. It ain't no different, Tiffany. It's all about wanting the outside of you to match what's on the inside.

TIFFANY. And what's inside of *you*, Eliza? A high-toned lady what goes to have tea with her friends and eats lettuce sandwiches? I don't think so. I've seen you at the dog tracks hootin' and hollerin' with all them tobacco-toothed friends of yourn. And I've seen you kickin' up your boots at your cowboy club and I've seen you prayin' hard and singin' loud and pushin' your arms up in the air to touch the hem of Jesus at that Piney Woods Bible-thumpin' church. What's inside of you is a country girl, Eliza – ain't no doubt about it, and you're always gonna *be* a country girl, no matter how good you learn to talk. Just like I'm gonna be T-Box right in here...

(touches her heart)

...where it counts the most.

(*ELIZA considers this. She gets up from the couch and starts toward the back of the apartment.*)

TIFFANY. What 'chu doin', sugar?

ELIZA. This way you got me lookin', Tiffany – it ain't who I am inside. I cain't go out on a date with Freddy lookin' like this.

TIFFANY. I think you're gorgeous lookin' thataway.

ELIZA. I may be beautiful to you, Tiffy. But I don't feel beautiful to myself. And I'll bet Freddy ain't gonna cotton to it neither.

(*ELIZA goes.*)

TIFFANY. (*apostrophizing Eliza, but to herself*) You'd be surprised what fellers cotton to. I should know. I used to be one.

(*The doorbell rings.* TIFFANY *calls to the back.*)

It's Freddy! Oh Lord! I'll keep him occupied till you can get yourself lookin' the way you like.

(*to herself, a grumble*)

Excuse me for takin' a little interest.

(*She goes to the "door" and admits not Freddy, but* CAL PICKERING.)

CAL. Hello, Tiffany.

TIFFANY. (*surprise*) Oh.

CAL. You look disappointed to see me.

TIFFANY. No, I ain't disappointed. I was just expectin' to see Freddy. He's comin' to pick up Eliza. They's goin' out.

CAL. So this is a bad time?

TIFFANY. It probably ain't the *best* time, sugar.

CAL. I think you've been avoiding me, Miss Tiffany Box.

TIFFANY. Now why would you think a thing like that?

(*CAL moves through the apartment. His body language says that he doesn't plan on leaving right away.*)

CAL. Because I've been trying to see you for two weeks now, without – maybe you've noticed? – *success.*

TIFFANY. *(unconvincingly)* I've been very busy.

CAL. Too busy to set aside a few minutes for your new friend Cal?

TIFFANY. I didn't know that we was friends.

CAL. I'd *like* to be your friend. Let's put it that way.

TIFFANY. I ain't got time for friends. I ain't even got much time for *myself* these days.

CAL. What do you do that keeps you so busy?

TIFFANY. Buncha things if you gotta know. There's this club in midtown where I wait on tables and sometimes I make drinks and sing a little. And I help Eliza with her pork rind business. And there's maybe a half dozen other things I do – whatever brings in a little extra money that won't get me arrested.

CAL. Are you strapped?

TIFFANY. What you mean, strapped?

CAL. For cash.

TIFFANY. Who ain't? I mean, ceptin' well-off folk like you.

CAL. Do you need money?

TIFFANY. I don't need *your* money.

CAL. What's wrong with *my* money?

TIFFANY. Professor Pickering –

CAL. Please call me Cal.

TIFFANY. Cal. You're a nice man and all, I got no doubt about that. But I ain't the kind of girl you think I am.

CAL. Everybody has skeletons, Tiffany. Some closets are bigger than others.

TIFFANY. Mine's a doublewide, honey, and I don't feel much like revealin' all my secrets to somebody new right now.

CAL. *(crushed)* I understand. I had hoped for reciprocity, but I knew there was a good chance that –

TIFFANY. Reci—what?

CAL. That you might not return my feelings. That maybe this was the reason you kept avoiding my calls.

TIFFANY. That ain't it, Cal. Now you do appear to be a really...nice man.

CAL. *(with her)* "Nice man." Right. But I'm also a forty-eight year-old man with a bad knee that sometimes puts him totally out of commission. And I snore. Or so I've been told. I'm a geography teacher with a fear of long distance travel, so I spend a lot of vicarious hours with my atlases and my *National Geographics*. But even men like me –

TIFFANY. *(interrupting)* Ain't you never been married? Ain't you never even had a girlfriend?

CAL. I'm not Mr. Chips, if that's what you're wondering.

TIFFANY. Mr. Chips?

CAL. *Goodbye, Mr. Chips.* It's the story of a bookish, introverted school teacher whose life is suddenly invigorated by romance with a young woman quite his opposite.

TIFFANY. You ain't never had nobody come into your life like that before?

CAL. No.

(beat)

I've had – there have been – women. There have been short – very short – there have been the occasional –

TIFFANY. Hookers?

CAL. No, Tiffany. I do not descend to hookers. But I do, on occasion, find myself in the midst of the most ephemeral trysts.

TIFFANY. Ephem–?

CAL. *(explaining)* Last call. Ports in the proverbial storm.

TIFFANY. And what am *I*, Cal? A port in the storm? Is that what you think I am?

CAL. Not at all. You're different from every other girl I've ever met. And that's what I'm trying to –

TIFFANY. *(interrupting him again)* I'm different, Cal, because I ain't a girl at all.

(She lifts her wig à la Jack Lemmon in Some Like it Hot.*)*

At least not yet.

(CAL is struck speechless. It is obvious that he truly thought that Tiffany was a woman.)

Oh you can't be serious. You had to have suspected. I'm not *that* good, sugar.

(CAL shakes his head slowly, still in shock.)

Well, ain't you the most precious man I ever met! You bought it! I sold it and you bought it!

CAL. *(finally finding his voice)* What did you mean by "not yet"?

TIFFANY. I aim to get myself an operation when I can afford it.

CAL. An operation?

TIFFANY. To make myself a woman. Through and through. It's a very expensive procedure.

CAL. You want a sex change?

TIFFANY. Hello! Ain't you been listenin'?

(CAL nods.)

You're lookin' at me like I done told you I like to throw kittens off the rooftop.

CAL. No, I just –. I think I need a little time to process this.

TIFFANY. *(with a sudden edge)* You go and process then, honey. You process to your heart's delight.

CAL. I'll call you.

TIFFANY. *(with sarcasm)* I'm sure you will.

(She leads CAL to the door.)

CAL. Goodbye.

TIFFANY. Goodbye.

(He goes. Sotto voce:)

And good riddance.

(She takes a moment to compose herself, then puts her wig back on. ELIZA *comes out. She wears jeans and a nice blouse. The face paint is gone. She looks very nice, her beauty softly accented.)*

ELIZA. What happened?

TIFFANY. *(straightening her wig)* I just found out what side of Calvin Pickering's bread's got all the butter.

ELIZA. He didn't know?

*(*TIFFANY *shakes her head.)*

TIFFANY. Poor fool.

(thought shift)

Let me look at you. You look like a libarian. *(note: lib*ar*ian, not li*brar*ian)*

ELIZA. Good. I *want* to look like a libarian.

TIFFANY. *(examining Eliza's face)* You sure I can't touch you up with a little more blush and maybe just a dab of that sparkly purple eyeliner you liked so much on me last week?

ELIZA. *(gently)* It looked good on *you,* Tiffy. I don't think it's gonna look so good on *me.*

TIFFANY. *(capitulating)* All right. You're the boss. Just don't ever let me catch you wearin' a bun.

*(*ELIZA *smiles. Lights fade out.)*

Scene Two

(Lights come up on four different small tables in four separate areas of the stage. It should be indicated from the set decoration that these tables are all located in different restaurants. At one table sit **CLARA** *and her sister* **VICKI***; at another* **CAL** *and a* **MAN** *dressed in a waiter's uniform; at a third,* **FREDDY** *and* **ELIZA** *[Eliza wearing what she wore in the last scene]. The fourth table is empty. Light narrows on this last table. A* **HOSTESS** *leads* **IDA** *and* **HENRY** *to it.* **IDA** *and* **HENRY** *sit; the* **HOSTESS** *gives them menus, then exits.*

IDA. *(to* **HENRY***, looking around)* It's really quite nice and I'm almost certain I've never been here before.

HENRY. I'm glad you like it. I eat here three, four times a week. One of my various bachelor haunts.

IDA. So tell me. How are things going?

HENRY. Oh.

> *(beat)*

You're not one for small talk, are you?

IDA. My husband was very straightforward – cut right to the meat of things. I guess that it rubbed off on me. Do you think she's making progress? I must admit that I'm not seeing much improvement. I made this discovery during her visit to my house yesterday.

HENRY. What happened?

IDA. Genevieve, my new cook, had made stuffed salmon, dressed up so beautifully. Eliza took one look at the platter and cried "Whoo, doggie! That's what I call cookin'!"

HENRY. "Whoo doggie"?

> *(***IDA** *nods.)*

Was she drunk?

IDA. We'd had a cocktail.

HENRY. There you have it.

IDA. There I have what?

HENRY. She wasn't herself.

(long beat)

Who am I kidding?

*(**IDA** looks at **HENRY** in silence, waiting for him to continue.)*

The experiment is a failure, Ida. You said it yourself – you've seen little improvement. I've been gauging her progress for two weeks now and I don't think I've made even a dent in that hardscrabble accent of hers. And it isn't just the accent. It's the whole package – the hick colloquialisms, the whole country-fried Minnie Pearl/Britney Spears persona.

IDA. Britney Spears! Oh Henry, don't be *offensive!*

HENRY. After all the drills I've been putting her through, and the constant corrections. I keep waiting for that Helen-Keller-at-the-water-pump moment and it never happens. I – I just don't think I'm getting through to her.

IDA. Perhaps it will take more time than we thought.

HENRY. Or perhaps...

(importantly)

...perhaps deep down I don't *want* her to change.

IDA. Intriguing.

HENRY. Your son seems to be quite happy with her just the way she is. Maybe I am too.

IDA. Perhaps I should be added to that list as well. I find her colloquialisms charming. They give her color. May I tell you how many drab, colorless people fill my life? Far too many. And I include my own daughter Vicki. There are very few people in my world who fascinate me, Henry – who make me smile, who remind me that this planet is a very large and wonderfully diverse place. I need more people in my life like Eliza. And Gerald – he's my pool-boy. He wears a nipple ring. And *you,* Henry. You interest me too.

HENRY. I do?

IDA. You're stodgy and oh-so-proper and professorial on the outside, but deep within the recesses of your being, I just know that there's a free-wheeling adventurer just aching to break out and have himself –

HENRY. An adventure?

IDA. Good Lord, Henry. You're filthy rich – richer than even *me* and look at you: you've done nothing with your money that would even raise an eyebrow. My daughter Vicki would be so approving of you.

HENRY. I take it that's not the sort of approval I should be looking for.

IDA. But it's there. Inside you. A whole palette of wonderful, beautiful colors. As for Eliza – I was already beginning to think that you should like nothing better than to send her out the door hardly changed at all. Despite your frustration over her misuse of this language you love so much. Of course the lower classes misuse and abuse it! That's what lower classes do. But you never struck me as someone who despised them for it. You only wish that we all used language to a greater, more expressive extent. That each of us pushed the limits of our own life potential. I see that. But for every lazy kid who communicates in text-message shorthand and instant message emoticons, we can, no doubt, find someone even on the margins of society who has done amazing, transcendent things with their personal means of expression. Artists who speak with their paintbrushes, composers who speak with their music.

HENRY. But Eliza had hoped to use language as *her* means of expression.

IDA. But she already does, Henry. In her own way, and do we really want her to end up sounding like you and me? Maybe we don't. Maybe you're right; deep down we don't want her changed at all.

HENRY. But what if *she* wants to change? Let's not lose sight of what it is that *Eliza* wants. And to that end, I could really be letting her down. And I don't know what to do about it.

IDA. And for the present, neither do I. But it's too early to close the book on it, Henry. Here, have a breadstick.

(HENRY *takes the breadstick.* IDA *picks up her own. The two chomp and think. Lights shift to another table where* CLARA *and her sister* VICKI *sit. A* WAITER *is taking their orders.*)

VICKI. *(to the* WAITER. *Handing him her menu)* Just the house salad. And a Diet Coke. And I'm in a great hurry, so please do what you can to get us served as quickly as possible.

WAITER. We have Diet Pepsi.

VICKI. That's all very interesting, but I'd like a Diet Coke. Perhaps you've heard of it; it's like Coke, but it's diet.

WAITER. Ma'am, we only serve Diet Pepsi.

VICKI. Why?

CLARA. *(embarrassed)* Does it really matter, Vicki? Let it go.

VICKI. It matters to *me*. I want a Diet Coke.

(to the WAITER*)*

Please bring me a Diet Coke.

WAITER. *(seriously – he's a very accommodating waiter)* There's a Quicky Mart down the street. Maybe I could run over there.

VICKI. I don't care how you do it. Just hurry. I have to leave in thirty minutes.

WAITER. Yes ma'am.

(turning to CLARA*)*

And you ma'am.

CLARA. *(handing him her menu)* I'll have a Pepsi. And a B-L-T, with the sweet potato fries.

WAITER. Thank you, ma'am.

(He picks up the menus and goes.)

CLARA. Sometimes, Vicki, you can be so rude.

VICKI. There is no reason for not giving a customer what she wants.

CLARA. Yes there is. There are a lot of reasons. Some restaurants give you Cokes and some restaurants give you Pepsis and you need to learn how to just roll with it. The whole world has to roll with things. Why are you so special?

VICKI. Is this why you wanted to talk to me? So I can be lectured to?

CLARA. No.

(beat, as she marshals her thoughts)

I know what you were planning to do. I overheard you getting advice from one of your friends. I called Eliza to warn her, but she hasn't gotten back to me.

VICKI. Well, I was too late – at least for round one. I've had to postpone my chat with our brother's new trailer-trash hussy girlfriend until *after* their first – and hopefully, *only* date. But she's still going to get an earful.

CLARA. And why? Why does Eliza deserve an earful from you? What has she done wrong except that she happens to have been born into the wrong family on the wrong side of the tracks? Why should you go after her for something she has absolutely no control over?

VICKI. I could care less who she is or *what* she is, but that girl has no right to intrude upon our family. To bring the shame of her deficient life into *our* lives. The same thing happened to Aunt Katherine, if you recall. She married that ex-wrestler and suddenly, one whole branch of our extended family became personas non grata. Snubbed by the Wimpole Garden Guild. No more invitations to the Cotton Factor's ball. I refuse to let this happen to us. No trash is coming into this house that isn't going to be promptly carried out in Hefty Bags by the maid.

CLARA. First of all, Sis, Eliza isn't trash. She's just country. And what kind of reputation do you think our precious family is holding on to anyway? We've been a nonconformist bunch since we were in diapers. This whole idea that we've got some kind of societal standing is a total fabrication.

VICKI. I realize that we've fallen a little short over the last few years, but I will not stand by and watch us all sink into the gutter. I plan to marry well, even if you do not. And no man of any importance in this town is going to cast even a glance in my direction while our brother chases after a pig farmer's daughter.

CLARA. So what do you intend to do – pay her to go away?

VICKI. *(almost serious)* Or have her killed. I haven't quite decided yet.

CLARA. Were you born an awful person, Vicki, or did you become that way over time?

VICKI. I don't have to sit here and take this from you.

(She stands.)

CLARA. If you leave now, Vicki, that poor waiter will have gone all the way over to that Quicky-Mart for nothing.

VICKI. That isn't my problem.

CLARA. It *is* your problem, you thoughtless bitch.

(grabbing **VICKI** *by the arm)*

Now sit here and shut up and drink your Coke and eat your salad, and let's pretend that we're loving sisters if only for the next thirty minutes.

(With a snort of displeasure, **VICKI** *falls back into her seat. Lights shift to the third table occupied by* **CAL** *and a* **WAITER.** *)*

CAL. Thank you for talking to me, Chad.

CHAD THE WAITER. No problem, Professor Pickering. I was officially off the clock ten minutes ago.

CAL. I'm not your instructor anymore, Chad. You can call me Cal.

CHAD. Sure.

CAL. Are you hungry? Can I order you anything to eat?

CHAD. *(shaking his head)* I ate before my shift. What was it you wanted to talk to me about?

CAL. Well, it's a little hard to get into.

CHAD. Ease into any way you like, Prof – I mean, Cal. I'm easy.

CAL. You're gay, right?

CHAD. *(nodding, curious)* Are you about to come out to me, Cal?

CAL. Of course not. I mean, no, that isn't the issue here. Chad, do you know anybody – perhaps in your own circle of friends and acquaintances – a man who, let us say, is not all that happy being a man – who would like, instead, to be a woman?

CHAD. You mean like "Trannies"? Transgenders? Sure. I have a friend like that.

CAL. And is there to be a surgery at some point?

CHAD. At some point. She's not as gung-ho about the surgery as some trannies are. Everybody's different. So, Cal – did you fall in love with a trannie? Is that what this is all about?

CAL. I don't know. I'm still processing it.

CHAD. It's a bitch, isn't it?

CAL. What's a bitch?

CHAD. The human heart. Not a lot of hard and fast rules.

CAL. Yeah.

CHAD. You're a straight man, right?

CAL. Right.

CHAD. And you fell in love with another man.

CAL. I wouldn't put it that way.

CHAD. Then let me put it *this* way: you fell in love with a woman who just happens to be trapped inside a man's body.

CAL. Okay, that sounds right.

CHAD. And you don't know what to do about it.

CAL. I don't know what to do about it, you're right.

CHAD. Well, I can't tell you what to do, Cal. Most men like you – they wouldn't have even felt comfortable talking to *anybody* about it. 'Probably would have tried to

forget the whole thing – taken themselves a long hunt-
ing trip in the woods or parked themselves in front of
the tube to watch NASCAR on the Speed network –
anything to convince themselves that they're still real
men.

CAL. I don't watch NASCAR. I've been meaning to, though.

CHAD. You're missing my point, Professor.

CAL. No, no. I respect your point. And I thank you for your
time. The human heart is a complicated organ, you're
right.

CHAD. Let me get you a beer. We've got some great lagers
here.

(CAL *nods. Lights fade out here and come up on* ELIZA
and FREDDY. FREDDY *is eating a fancy-bread sandwich;* ELIZA *a pasta dish.*)

ELIZA. I like Alfredo.

FREDDY. It's good, huh? My dad liked it so much, my
mother was afraid he was going to try to stick me with
the name "Alfred" when I was born. I still think "Fred-
erick" was her way of nipping this in the bud.

ELIZA. *(licking her upper lip)* It's really creamy.

FREDDY. The best Fettuccine alfredo usually is. You should
have gotten it with the shrimp. Although that might
have been gilding the lily. I'm madly in love with you,
by the way, and I can't stop thinking about you.

ELIZA. Oh.

FREDDY. You invade my dreams.

ELIZA. I do?

FREDDY. These last two weeks have been torture.

ELIZA. They have?

FREDDY. I'm glad you finally agreed to go out with me. I'm
so glad you came into my life.

ELIZA. You are?

FREDDY. You sound like you don't know what to say.

ELIZA. I don't.

FREDDY. Is that bad?

ELIZA. No. I reckon not.

FREDDY. Is this happening too fast? Am I coming on too strong? I sometimes come on too strong. I'm impulsive. My father was impulsive. I guess I'm a chip off the old block.

ELIZA. Freddy, I don't know what to say. I hardly know you. I *like* you. But I hardly know you.

FREDDY. I'll take "like." Like is good. Like is a good start. I should shut up. I'm babbling. It's just that when I look at you –

ELIZA. What about when you *listen* to me? Don't my voice, don't my way of talkin' make you kinda, kinda –

FREDDY. Kinda what? I love the way you talk, Eliza. I can't believe you're letting Henry Higgins alter that wonderful down-home, good-country-people way you have of expressing yourself. It's the best thing about you.

ELIZA. The way I talk – that's the best thing about me?

FREDDY. Well, *one* of the best things. One of the things I love.

ELIZA. *(trying to understand)* Do you love me just 'cuz you love me or do you love me 'cuz you maybe always wanted to fall in love with a country girl?

FREDDY. I don't – [understand]

ELIZA. Like the way you was lookin' at me the first time we met. Was it 'cuz I wasn't like nobody else you ever knew? Was that why you smiled at me so much?

FREDDY. You're different, I'll admit it.

ELIZA. And you like it that I'm different?

FREDDY. I like it that you're *you.* And if being different is part of the package, then so be it.

ELIZA. Freddy, my pa always had them birddogs what he'd take huntin' with him in the fall. And one day this li'l old mutt puppy shows up on our porch, small enough you could hold in your hand, and it don't look like it's gonna grow up into anything but a mutt and a small runty mutt at that. And Freddy, my pa, who probably never paid no never-mind to no dog in his life, ceptin' his birddogs, and they was like *employees* to him, why he looked at that little no-account puppy what got left behind by her mama, kicked away from her motherly teat for being so small and so ugly lookin' and he looked at that helpless little thing and he smiled so big you could see pert near every tooth in his head and he raised that little girl like she was gonna grow up to be the best dog a man ever had, and I swear, Freddy, that's just the way you've been lookin' at me since we met. Like I'm your own little runt-puppy you're gonna take care of and love for no other reason than maybe you like to give a little of your heart to somebody you think needs the givin'. But that ain't no way to fall in love. It's pity-love, Freddy. And it ain't the kind of love I cotton to.

FREDDY. It ain't pity-love, Eliza.

ELIZA. You said "ain't."

FREDDY. I did?

ELIZA. Yep, you surely did. Are you makin' fun of me on top of everything else?

FREDDY. No, no! It must have just slipped out.

ELIZA. It ain't a good word: ain't. It says a person don't got self-respect. *You* got self-respect. You got no cause at all to be sayin' that word. You leave that word to people like me.

FREDDY. It doesn't matter how you talk, Eliza. I just want to be with you.

ELIZA. Like my pa wanted to be with that puppy. I cain't have you treatin' me like that puppy, Freddy. I wanna be like one of them birddogs. I wanna stand all proud and pointy in the field. I ain't no runty-mutt-puppy! Goodbye, Freddy.

(**ELIZA** *gets up and storms off. Blackness spreads across the stage.*)

Scene Three

(Lights come up on Henry Higgins' classroom. **HENRY** *sits alone at his desk, lost in troubled thought. After a moment,* **CAL** *steps inside.* **HENRY** *glances up and nods a silent greeting.)*

HENRY. How'd you know where I'd be?

CAL. You weren't at your house or in your office.

HENRY. Sometimes I walk. I wander the campus.

CAL. *I* just got through wandering the campus myself. I didn't see you. Freddy Hill wants to talk to you. He said you haven't returned his calls.

HENRY. I can't help Freddy. I can't help Eliza. I can't even help myself.

CAL. Well, you'd better think of something to say to him because he's on his way over here too.

HENRY. She didn't show up. We were supposed to have a lesson tonight. Nine o'clock. She didn't show. I don't think she's coming back. How was your date with Tiffany?

CAL. *(distracted)* Oh. Yes. Non-existent. Tiffany isn't a Tiffany. I talked to someone at the club where she works. Tiffany's real name is Roger Bosco. Did you know that "she" was really a "he"?

*(***HENRY** *nods.)*

Why is the straight guy with a misplaced gender-confused crush always the last one to know?

HENRY. Ida says I'm not being true to myself. She thinks there is someone inside of me I've never even met before. How did we get ourselves into this fix, Calvin? I made the innocent suggestion that we go to the Tri-Counties Fair and Livestock Show this year and here we are mired in bewildered introspection and feeling utterly miserable.

CAL. Maybe we were always miserable and we never knew it.

(Now **FREDDY** *steps into the classroom.)*

FREDDY. *(to* **HENRY***)* There you are.

HENRY. You ferreted me out.

FREDDY. *(looking around, frowning)* This place is bleak. You've got nothing on your walls.

HENRY. What would you like to see, Freddy? Construction-paper cut-outs of Thanksgiving turkeys? This is college.

FREDDY. At this point in time, seeing the inside of a neighborhood pub would be my strongest preference. Let me buy you both a beer.

CAL. I'm game. Will the TV over the bar be turned to the Speed Channel?

FREDDY. *(playfully hopeful)* Who knows? Maybe you'll get lucky.

(The **THREE MEN** *cross to a bar counter representing a neighborhood watering hole. They sit down on three vacant stools, which conveniently place them facing the audience downstage. A* **BARTENDER** *takes their orders in pantomime. At the same time, lights come up over* **IDA***'s terrace.* **IDA** *and* **CLARA** *are having a drink.)*

IDA. You should carry a can of Diet Coke in your purse, honey. Next time that happens, just whip it out and save the day.

CLARA. I mention it to make a point, Mama.

IDA. I got the point years ago, sweetie. I got the point the day Vicki pulled her baby-sized pucker away from my lactating breast and asked in so many words why we didn't employ a wetnurse.

CLARA. *(laughing)* Oh Mama, she didn't!

*(***IDA** *grins. Now* **VICKI** *steps out onto the terrace.)*

VICKI. *(dour)* Were you making fun of me just now?

IDA. Oh sweetie, we're *always* making fun of you.

VICKI. You're drunk.

IDA. Not yet. Soon, though.

VICKI. I hate it when the two of you get this way.

CLARA. What way, Vicki?

VICKI. Thinking everything is a great big joke. It gets on my nerves.

IDA. Vicki, honey, your sister and I do not find humor in *everything*. But it does help as we make our way through this sad ol' world – especially when certain meddlesome family members choose to throw obstacles in our path and make the going difficult – to find things along the way which make us smile, which lighten our step.

VICKI. I'm meddlesome? I throw things in your path?

IDA. Of course you do, honey. It's a vocation! And I really wish you would stop. I really wish that you would start being the girl who tries to brighten the lives of others for a change.

CLARA. You need to lighten your step, Vicki, and quit being such a snobby bitch.

VICKI. *(an angry defense)* Clara yanked my arm in a public place.

CLARA. I'm sorry I yanked your arm, but you were misbehaving.

VICKI. If I have no right to tell you and Mother what to do, you have no right to order *me* all about. This whole family is a mortifying embarrassment.

IDA. I'm sorry you feel that way, Vicki. People aren't deliberately going out of their way to mortify and embarrass you, darling, I can assure you.

VICKI. *Some* people do. That awful pig girl and her man-woman transvestite friend. I sent them away. I wouldn't let them set foot in this house.

IDA. When did you do this, honey?

VICKI. A few minutes ago. While you two were out here drinking up the family liquor cabinet.

IDA. They came asking to see me?

(VICKI nods.)

And you wouldn't let them in the house?

VICKI. I most certainly did not. Regardless of what you and Clara think of me, I am not ineffectual.

CLARA. *(jumping up, to* IDA*)* I'll try to find them. They couldn't have gone too far.

(Just as CLARA *starts to head inside,* ELIZA *and* TIF-FANY *enter from the side yard.)*

TIFFANY. Oh look, Eliza! They're here after all.

(waving at CLARA *and* IDA*)*

Haloooo! Haloooo!

(directed to IDA*)*

Your sullen daughter, Miss Vicki, said you weren't home.

CLARA. *(cheerily)* Thank you for joining us. We're having a nightcap. Or two.

IDA. Or three.

VICKI. You're all drunk. You're a disgrace.

IDA. *(to* ELIZA *and* TIFFANY *as they reach the terrace)* Vicki needs a drink. Clara, go make drinks for our guests and mix your sister something especially potent. We need to take the edge off of her.

*(*CLARA *steps inside the house.)*

(to VICKI*)*

You have an unbecoming edge, dear. Sit down.

*(*IDA *deposits* VICKI *in a chair.)*

TIFFANY. So this is what the rich and decadent do on a Friday night – get themselves all liquored up on the lanai.

IDA. Actually, this is a first.

(calling)

Isn't it, Clara?

(to TIFFANY*)*

But we thought it was high time. This family has been very tightly wound lately. I thought it would be a nice change for us to unwind together in a private and genteel setting.

(**CLARA** *steps out, holding a bottle of black cherry juice.*)

CLARA. Mama, what is this?

IDA. It's black cherry juice, dear.

CLARA. *(smirking)* And did someone tell you to drink it?

IDA. I think I read about it in *Prevention.* It's supposed to be good for gout, honey. Now run along before your head gets too big and explodes all over the terrace.

(**CLARA** *exits with a chuckle.*)

TIFFANY. *(to* **IDA***)* You have a lovely place here.

(to **ELIZA***)*

Don't she have a lovely place?

(**ELIZA** *nods.*)

Still not talkin'?

(to **IDA***, regarding* **ELIZA***)*

She ain't talked hardly atall since she got back from her date with your boy Freddy. I don't reckon it went well.

VICKI. *(rolling her eyes in disgust)* What are you – Tom Sawyer? "Reckon."

TIFFANY. *(ignoring this, to* **IDA***)* Maybe *you'd* have better luck gettin' her to say what went wrong.

IDA. *(tenderly, to* **ELIZA***)* Do you want to talk about it, sweetie?

ELIZA. Nothing really to say, ma'am. I like your son, I do. I just don't think he's the right one for me.

IDA. And why do you say this, dear?

VICKI. *(perking up)* She doesn't have to have a reason. She has a right to dislike Freddy for whatever reason suits her fancy.

IDA. *(to* **ELIZA***)* Does that suit you, honey? Thinking that Freddy might not be the right one for you?

(**ELIZA** *shakes her head.*)

Then tell me, darling. Tell me exactly what's wrong.

(The conversation continues in pantomime as we shift our attention to the saloon. During the following

exchange among the three men, **CLARA** *will deliver drinks to her terrace companions and each of the women will become either newly drunk or progressively drunker [such as the case may be]. The three* **MEN***, having had a head-start, are well on their own way to full and happy inebriety. Evidence of time passage are several empty beer bottles set before them on the bar.)*

HENRY. So, it's a deal then. Sunday morning, we're all going skydiving.

CAL. I thought tomorrow morning was the skydiving and Sunday morning was the bungee jumping.

FREDDY. Now I'm really confused. When is the hot-air ballooning?

HENRY. *(to* **FREDDY***)* So you've never even kissed her?

*(***FREDDY*** shakes his head.)*

How do you know that things won't change once you've planted that first kiss on her soft, sweet lips?

FREDDY. *(looking at* **HENRY** *with a curious eye)* Something in that question makes me wonder if you'd like to kiss her too, Henry.

HENRY. Of course I'd like to kiss her. We'd all like to kiss her. Bartender!

(The **BARTENDER** *comes over. To the bartender:)*

Would *you* like to kiss her?

BARTENDER. Kiss who?

CAL. Henry, for God's sake, he's never even met her.

BARTENDER. Who are we talking about?

CAL. Someone you don't know. Get me another beer will you?

FREDDY. Actually, he does know her. Don't you, Gerald?

BARTENDER. How do I know this woman?

FREDDY. You met her in my mother's backyard. By the pool.

(to **HENRY** *and* **CAL***)*

This is Gerald, by the way: Mom's pool-boy.

GERALD. *(shaking hands)* Hi. Nice to know you.

CAL. Then you must also know Eliza's friend "Tiffany."

GERALD. Yeah. I've known Tiff for quite a while. I tend bar at "Judy's Rainbow" sometimes. They're both nice girls. And yeah, I'd kiss Eliza. I'd do more than kiss her. She's hot. Am I offending anybody here?

FREDDY. I suppose not. You know that most of the members of my family think you're gay, don't you?

GERALD. Yeah. Them and a whole bunch of other people. Maybe it's because I tend bar at gay clubs and clean pools in my speedos. Now here's my opinion, and I know it's a little outside my job description to be doing more than just *listening* to your troubles, but I've been picking up a lot from the whole lot of you these last few days – out by the pool, making drinks here and at Tiffany's club. 'Been piecing it together bit by bit – been kinda fun, really. Now *you* –

(pointing to CAL)

Tiffany's boyfriend.

CAL. *(wild protest)* I am not Tiffany's –

GERALD. You want her. I can tell. Wait until after the surgery and see if you don't feel better about the whole thing. Go out on a limb for the first time. You college profs – you come in here all buttoned down and closed up and then I pour a little booze down your gullets and suddenly you're showing your true colors – and they aren't even bad colors, man. Okay, it's bad you gotta get yourself wasted to get in touch with what you're really feeling, but some day maybe you'll figure out some easier way to do it. Which means, Professor Higgins, that maybe it's time for you to pump up the volume on that predictable-as-hell bachelor's life of yours and start making some real noise around here – like how many times do I see you sitting back in that corner booth grading your papers and having your quiet lonely pint? Letting everything pass you by. Grab her while you have the chance – before all the life that's in you gets drained away.

HENRY. Grab *whom* while I have the chance?

FREDDY. *(suspiciously)* Yeah, who?

GERALD. Freddy's mom, you broken toasters. Ms. Hill.

  (to **HENRY***)*

  I've heard her talking about you, Professor. She really likes you.

HENRY. *(considering this)* We do have a rapport.

FREDDY. *(smiling)* Vicki would slit her wrists. A crusty academic for a stepfather. What's a college professor rate in the society register?

CAL. I know he ranks higher than a pool-boy.

  *(***GERALD*** frowns at this but doesn't respond.)*

HENRY. *(to* **FREDDY***)* She *is* a dear woman. Gout-free even.

FREDDY. *(to* **GERALD***)* And what about *me?*

GERALD. You?

FREDDY. Yeah. While you're playing matchmaker or therapist or whatever, where do *I* stand?

GERALD. Well, okay. Answer me this question: do you love Eliza?

FREDDY. Of course I do.

GERALD. For all the right reasons?

FREDDY. What are the right reasons?

HENRY. He means: Are you slumming, boy?

FREDDY. Of course I'm not slumming.

HENRY. Do you feel sorry for her?

FREDDY. Only insomuch as I want her to be happy, and I suspect that up to now her life hasn't been all that happy of one. Is it wrong for me to want better things for her than what she's had up to now? Is that pity? She thinks it's pity. But it can't be.

GERALD. Then I pronounce you all happy-ever-after.

  (This isn't so easily done: all **THREE MEN** *are immersed in their thoughts – sorting, "processing," as they wander out of the bar. Lights shift to the terrace.* **IDA, ELIZA, CLARA,** *and* **TIFFANY** *are standing over* **VICKI***.)*

TIFFANY. You'll love it. Won't she love it, girls?

(Nods all around.)

VICKI. I am *not* going skinny-dipping in that pool.

CLARA. Are you telling me that we rolled back the thermal bubble for nothing?

VICKI. You're being ridiculous. What if one of the neighbors happened to see?

IDA. We'll turn out the lights, dear. You need this. It will be good for all of us. But you have to go first.

TIFFANY. *(to* **VICKI***)* Because you're the most –

(turning to **CLARA***)*

What's the word?

CLARA. Repressed.

*(***TIFFANY** *nods and smiles.)*

VICKI. You think you can ply me with liquor and I'll let my guard down? Think again.

IDA. All right.

(to the others)

We tried.

(turning to **CLARA***)*

Clara, dear, call your brother. Tell him to come home. It's time for bed. The evening is over. We were all going to jump in the pool without our clothes on but it was not meant to be. And so now we will all crawl between our respective sheets and call it a night.

(She sits down.)

After one more nightcap.

(She holds her glass up to **CLARA** *who takes it.* **ELIZA** *goes to sit down next to* **IDA.** **IDA** *runs a hand through* **ELIZA***'s hair.)*

Eliza Doolittle, you have the silkiest, softest hair I've ever felt.

ELIZA. Thank you. I use Suave.

IDA. Did you know your mother, sweetie? How old were you when she died?

ELIZA. Five.

IDA. And do you remember her?

ELIZA. *(with a smile)* I got a few nice memories.

IDA. What kind of a woman was she?

ELIZA. Beautiful. Soft, sweet voice. She was purdy young. There was a big age difference between her and my pa.

IDA. But she was *like* your pa? Good solid stock?

ELIZA. I reckon you could say that.

IDA. And did she sound like your father? The way she talked – the way she put herself across.

ELIZA. No ma'am.

IDA. What do you mean?

TIFFANY. *(answering for Eliza)* Eliza's ma was from Boston, Ida. She met Liza's pa when she took a wrong turn on her way to a Delta blues festival.

IDA. I declare! What an interesting way to meet one's future husband.

TIFFANY. Her family disowned her, though – when them two got married. Didn't never ever come down and see her. Not the whole six years they was together before she died.

IDA. How terrible!

ELIZA. So I don't know much about that side of my family.

VICKI. *(to ELIZA)* How did she die?

TIFFANY. *(to ELIZA)* You want that I should tell her or do you want to?

ELIZA. No. I'll tell her. She was run over by a car.

TIFFANY. Tell her who was drivin' the car, Liza.

ELIZA. It was an encyclopedia salesman what did it. She was run over by a man what made his livin' off books and learnin'.

TIFFANY. What you have here is what they call a "life-irony."

IDA. How do you mean?

TIFFANY. Eliza's pa – see – he couldn't read when them two met. Her ma taught him how to read. 'Was teachin' him a lot of things up to the day she died. Educatin' him. Educatin' Eliza too. Then it all stopped.

ELIZA. Pa closed up all the books. Threw 'em all down into the fruit cellar. Let me go to school for a while, but never liked it. Finally he just pulled me right out. 'Kept the truant officer quiet with country ham.

IDA. That's awful!

ELIZA. I understood why he did it. It warn't a good reason in my book, but you see, it all reminded him too much of my ma – my getting' educated. It reminded him how smart she was and how well she read and how much he loved her and missed her. I loved my pa, still do. I didn't want to see him hurt so much, so I just gave up on tryin' to be like my mama.

IDA. But was it fair of him to hold you back, darling?

ELIZA. He ain't holdin' me back no more. I got to thinkin' that I have a right to be somethin' more than what he sees me bein'. We had us a good long talk a few months back and he came to see it my way. I ain't snea-kin' around with my lessons. He knows exactly what I'm doin'.

TIFFANY. But you still ain't lettin' yourself learn nothin', Liza. Deep down, you're still thinkin' it would hurt your pa. Or else why ain't Professor Higgins able to get nothin' through that country-fried skull of yours?

VICKI. *(to* **ELIZA***)* You aren't waiting for your father to die, are you?

CLARA. Vicki, that was uncalled for.

ELIZA. *(answering Vicki's question)* No.

(She thinks this over.)

Or it could be that's *exactly* what I'm waiting for. He's a good man. They's all good country people – Pa's people, *my* people – smart in their own way, even though they ain't got much money, don't got a lot of chances to make a better life for themselves. Why do

you think people in my part of the state started eatin'
pork rinds? Why, pork rinds ain't nothin' but fried pig
skin. Whoever thought of eatin' pig skin? Poor folk,
that's who. But they warn't *stupid* folk. They was smart
enough to figure a way to make a little money outa
somethin' nobody ever made money at before. And I
guess I just thought that I could be smart and read and
learn myself on my own and get by soundin' the way I
sound, but it ain't so easy to be taken seriously when
you sound like this. That's why I asked Professor Higgins to help me.

IDA. But he couldn't.

ELIZA. *(softly, confessional)* Yes he did.

*(She stands up. Suddenly her hick accent falls completely
away and she takes up the more educated, cultured
southern address of Henry and Cal and Ida Hill and
her three children. ELIZA holds her glass out to CLARA.)*

Clara, while you are filling your "last call" drink orders,
could you make me a Vodka stinger? I've always
wanted to try one. This is the night for trying things
we've never tried before – for starting new chapters,
for turning the page and discovering wonderful new
opportunities and wonderful new friends. I want to
toast this beautiful night of promise. To hope. To thou-
sands of glorious possibilities.

*(While ELIZA has been speaking with her back turned to
the house, and to the gape-mouthed surprise of the other
women, the three MEN arrive, drunk, a little unsteady
on their feet, but cogent and fairly-well focused. Now they
too register interest and amazement over Eliza's sudden
transformation.)*

FREDDY. To love?

(ELIZA turns. The two fall into each other's arms.)

ELIZA. And you'll love me still, even after I get my teeth
fixed?

(FREDDY nods.)

TIFFANY. This is so romantic, I think I'm gonna cry or shit or something.

FREDDY. *(to* **ELIZA***)* We – the three of us…

(indicating Henry and Cal and himself)

…were talking in the cab about how we wanted to jump-start our own lives – how we were going to get ourselves off that same page where we'd all been languishing for too long. I think at one point Cal considered running away with the circus.

*(***CAL*** shrugs.)*

But here's what we finally settled on and it involves you too, Eliza:

(He takes a steadying breath.)

We – the three of us – we're buying the Pig Palace. We're buying ourselves the best barbecue restaurant in Shawsville.

CAL. Shorty Joyner's been ready to retire for some time now. And his son – that would be *Little* Shorty – wants out of the barbecue business, so now would be the perfect time for us to make an offer.

ELIZA. That's a very nice restaurant. They change the sawdust on the floor almost every night.

FREDDY. *(nodding excitedly)* People from all over the world eat at that place. Henry can set himself up in a front booth and jot down every dialect on the planet. And we want you to be the hostess, Eliza – learn the ropes and in no time at all we'll promote you to manager.

ELIZA. *(in joyous shock)* I don't know what to say.

IDA. *(to* **ELIZA***)* You can say whatever you want to, angel. And in any *way* you care to say it. Talk like your dad if you like, or the Kennedys. Or maybe you can just talk like yourself – like that lovely southern woman who lives inside of you. I'll bet you've never tried *that* before.

*(***ELIZA*** nods and smiles.)*

CLARA. *(raising her glass)* I think we should celebrate.

HENRY. But not quite yet. Cal, you had something you wanted to say to Tiffany.

TIFFANY. *(to* **CAL***)* You gonna send me back to Kansas to be with Hunk and Zeke and Auntie Em?

CAL. No. I'm going to send you to a hospital to get your sexual reassignment surgery. If that's what you really want to do.

TIFFANY. *(stunned)* You're gonna pay for my operation?

CAL. If that's what you want.

TIFFANY. Of course it's what I want!

(She throws her arms around **CAL.***)*

It's all I've ever wanted.

(Her expression turning serious, hopeful.)

And after the surgery –

CAL. I don't know. It's a big leap for me. I still can't promise that –

TIFFANY. *(genuinely)* I understand. Ding dong! The boy is gone!

(She grins.)

CLARA. Vicki, have you anything to add to any of this?

VICKI. No. I'm just going to sit here in silence and nurse my gin and tonic until everything goes away.

(Long beat. It seems that there is something else that **VICKI** *wishes to say, struggling to push its way forward.)*

People come to that restaurant – that Pig Palace – all sorts of people?

FREDDY. It's been rated one of the best pork barbecue restaurants in the South. Emeril Lagasse was there last week with Rachael Ray.

CLARA. Rachael walked out with a barbecue-sauce clown mouth. It wasn't pretty.

VICKI. *(She's never thought about this before:)* So people with money go there? CEO's and millionaire athletes and owners of regional Toyota dealerships?

(Everyone answers Vicki with a nod. **VICKI** *smiles – for perhaps the first time in the play.)*

FREDDY. So we're all good?

HENRY. We're all good. One of us would be even better, though, if Ida would let him take her out to dinner. I should also mention: there's wrestling at the coliseum on Monday night.

IDA. Wrestling?

HENRY. I've been doing a little research. It's really quite popular. Soap opera for men, they call it.

IDA. It does sound – *intriguing.*

*(***HENRY** *smiles and places an affectionate hand upon her arm.)*

CAL. There is one tiny fly in the ointment of this evening.

(All eyes are now on **CAL.***)*

Early tonight we learned some disturbing news – for those who care about such things.

(All heads lean in.)

Apparently straight men wear nipple rings too.

IDA. Calvin Pickering, what are you talking about?

FREDDY. Gerald the pool-boy isn't gay, Mom. He's as straight as they come.

*(***VICKI** *gets up from her chair. She moves away from her companions, and closes her eyes in private rapture.)*

VICKI. Mother, I think I detected a little rip in the thermal bubble. You really should get Gerald back over here to check that out. And soon.

CLARA. Yes, Mama. Very, very soon.

(Lights fade out as **VICKI** *and* **CLARA** *trade blissful, companionable smiles.)*

End of Play

PROPERTIES LIST

ACT ONE Scene One
>Four "hamburger plates" and accompanying beverages
>Henry's notebook and pen
>Bags of homemade pork rinds affixed to shoulder sticks

ACT ONE Scene Two
>Assorted newspapers
>Juice glass with a little orange juice left in it
>Coffee cup
>Breakfast dishes
>Clear-away tray
>Glass of pink lemonade

ACT ONE Scene Three
>Chalk
>Eraser
>Eliza's notebook and pen

ACT TWO Scene One
>Tiffany's partially-eaten sandwich upon a plate
>Tiffany's cell phone

ACT TWO Scene Two
>**IDA & HENRY:** Two menus, napkins, silverware, container of breadsticks
>**VICKI & CLARA:** Two menus, napkins, silverware
>**ELIZA & FREDDY:** "Fancy bread" sandwich on a plate, pasta in a bowl, napkins, silverware, beverages

ACT TWO Scene Three
>Five cocktails
>Several empty beer bottles

COSTUME LIST

ACT ONE Scene One

YOUNG MAN: jeans, t-shirt, cowboy boots, baseball cap
YOUNG WOMAN: jeans, peasant blouse, sandals
OLDER MAN: bib overalls, large t-shirt, straw hat, cowboy boots
OLDER WOMAN: floral apron dress, white sneakers
FREDDY HILL: khaki pants, polo shirt, loafers
CLARA HILL: white pedal-pushers, brightly-colored blouse, white sandals
IDA HILL: brightly-colored pants, light floral jacket, white sandals
HENRY HIGGINS: tweed jacket with elbow patches, dress shirt, dress pants, plaid bow tie, loafers
CAL PICKERING: Polo shirt, khaki pants, loafers
ELIZA DOOLITTLE: Gingham shirt, jeans, sneakers
TIFFANY BOX: black velveteen midrift tank, purple sequined sweater, hot pants with fishnet overlay leggings, high heels, over-sized jewelry

ACT ONE Scene Two

IDA: paisley lounging gown, metallic slippers
OPAL: maid's uniform
CLARA: tennis dress, sneakers
FREDDY: jogging outfit, running shoes
VICKI HILL: tennis outfit, sneakers
ELIZA: pastel blouse, jeans, sneakers

ACT ONE Scene Three

HENRY: red plaid button-down shirt, dark brown bow tie, tweed jacket with elbow patches, brown dress pants, loafers
IDA: sweater set, skirt, pumps
CAL: argyle sweater vest, Oxford cloth shirt, dress pants, loafers
ELIZA: same as last scene: pastel blouse, jeans, sneakers

ACT TWO Scene One

TIFFANY: short dress with wide black belt, floral scarf, jeweled denim jacket, metallic stockings, sling-back shoes, jewelry
ELIZA: *before change:* psychedelic print shirt, belt, denim mini-skirt, hot pink leggings, high heels, large earrings
after change: embroidered peasant blouse, jeans, strappy sandals
CAL: dress shirt and tie, black pants, dress shoes

ACT TWO Scene Two

CLARA: dress skirt, blouse, jacket, pumps

VICKI: two-piece suit (skirt, jacket), pumps

CAL: same as last scene: dress shirt and tie, black pants, dress shoes

CHAD: black t-shirt, pants, belt

FREDDY: Oxford cloth shirt, khaki pants, loafers

ELIZA: same as last scene: embroidered peasant blouse, jeans, strappy sandals

RESTAURANT HOSTESS: dark skirt, white shirt

IDA: evening wear suit, pumps, tasteful jewelry

HENRY: dark suit, white shirt, dark bow tie, dress shoes

CLARA & VICKI's WAITER: white shirt, dark pants

ACT TWO Scene Three

HENRY: dark sports jacket, white shirt, khaki pants, dark bow tie, loafers

CAL: Polo shirt, dark pants, loafers

FREDDY: Hawaiian shirt, chinos, sneakers

GERALD: tight t-shirt, jeans, loafers

IDA: tropical muumuu, leggings, sandals

CLARA: beach dress (and bare feet)

VICKI: two-piece sleeveless top and skirt set, flats

ELIZA: sweatshirt, jeans, sneakers

TIFFANY: brown fringed skirt, with jeweled blouse and belt

Also by
Mark Dunn...

Belles

Cabin Fever: A Texas Tragicomedy

A Delightful Quarantine

Dix Tableaux

Five Tellers Dancing in the Rain

Gendermat

Helen's Most Favorite Day

Judge and Jury

Minus Some Buttons

Mrs. Townely Had a Pomeranian

Sand Pies and Scissorlegs

Please visit our website **samuelfrench.com** for complete
descriptions and licensing information.

MORE AVAILABLE FROM
SAMUEL FRENCH

A DELIGHTFUL QUARANTINE
Mark Dunn

Comedy / 5m,10f, 2 extras (girls) / Simple Sets

What would it be like to be confined with people you don't really know? Strange visitors leave behind a deadly disease that leaves seven separate households unexpectedly quarantined. Seven story lines are deftly balanced as people are forced to confront their personal issues. A heart-warming original comedy/drama about how people react when there's nowhere else to go.

"Sharp and witty, warm and very, very funny."
–*Williamsport Sun-Gazette*